Praise for Thomas Bernhard's *WALKING*

"The point of view that found devastating expression in masterpieces like *Concrete* and *Yes* is already apparent. What is extraordinary about Bernhard is that his relentless pessimism never seems open to ridicule; his world is so powerfully imagined that it can seem to surround you like little else in literature."

The New Yorker

"We lose ourselves into madness, we find, not at the end of reason's course but in the infinity between two beats of reason's clock. It is Bernhard's genius to be able to make this revelation darkly, but giddily, humorous. Kenneth Northcott's translation brilliantly renders the drama of this piece. . . . *Walking* has the uncompromising force of Bernhard's mature fiction."

THOMAS SIMPSON, *Chicago Tribune*

"It is with *Walking* that we understand how Bernhard's writing . . . is a consistent, desperate, humorous, bitter, and all-too-human attempt to keep from going under."

JEFFREY DESHELL, *Review of Contemporary Fiction*

"Entering Bernhard's world means suspending the tyranny of good taste, conventional wishes, and the false comforts of the consumerist lifestyle. It means entering a realm of thoughtful perversity whose antecedents include Rabelais, Jonathan Swift, Nikolay Gogol, and Dostoevsky's *Underground Man*."

STEVE DOWDEN, *World and I*

"[Bernhard is] one of the masters of contemporary European fiction."

GEORGE STEINER

WALKING

TRANSLATED BY KENNETH J. NORTHCOTT
WITH A FOREWORD BY BRIAN EVENSON

WALKING

A NOVELLA

THOMAS BERNHARD

The University of Chicago Press *Chicago and London*

THOMAS BERNHARD (1931–1989) was an Austrian playwright, novelist, and poet. English translations of his works published by the University of Chicago Press include *The Voice Imitator* (1997), translated by Kenneth J. Northcott; *Woodcutters* (1987) and *Wittgenstein's Nephew* (1988), translated by David McLintock; and *Histrionics* (1990), three plays translated by Peter Jansen and Kenneth J. Northcott.

The University of Chicago Press, Chicago 60637
The University of Chicago Press, Ltd., London

Printed in the United States of America

Published originally by The University of Chicago in a collection with two other novellas, *Amras* and *Playing Watten*.

Walking was first published in German as *Gehen*,

24 23 22 21 20 19 18 17 16 15 1 2 3 4 5

ISBN-13: 978-0-226-31104-3 (paper)
ISBN-13: 978-0-226-31118-0 (e-book)
DOI: 10.7208/chicago/9780226311180.001.0001

Library of Congress Cataloging-in-Publication Data

Bernhard, Thomas, author.
[Gehen. English]
Walking : a novella / Thomas Bernhard ; translated by Kenneth J. Northcott ; with a foreword by Brian Evenson.
pages ; cm
ISBN 978-0-226-31104-3 (pbk. : alk. paper) — ISBN 978-0-226-31118-0 (ebook)
I. Northcott, Kenneth J., translator. II. Evenson, Brian, 1966– writer of foreword.
III. Title.
PT2662.E7G413 2015
833'.914—dc23

2015004418

⊗ This paper meets the requirements of ANSI/NISO Z39.48-1992 (Permanence of Paper).

FOREWORD

"The feeling grows that Thomas Bernhard is now the most original, concentrated novelist writing in German," wrote George Steiner while the Austrian writer Thomas Bernhard was still alive. Now, more than two decades after his death, it has become increasingly clear that Bernhard was one of the strongest voices of twentieth-century European fiction, on an equal standing with writers such as Franz Kafka, Samuel Beckett, and Robert Musil. Possessed of an eccentric syntax and an incomparably rhythmical prose style, Bernhard's best-known works function as irony-ridden monologues and screeds against his native Austria. They submerge readers deep within a maddened or evasive or sophistic voice and hold them there, not allowing them to come to the textual surface for air. Bernhard's sense of these voices is impeccable and unrelenting. Their habitual patterns of expression are so strong that to read Bernhard is to feel as if you have been possessed, as if the thoughts of others are worming their way into your skull and changing the way you parse and categorize the world. As the sentences stack up and logic begins a relentless and darkly comic spin, you are in danger of being crowded out of your own head. This is a dilemma shared by Bernhard's characters as well: "Since my thinking had actually been Roithamer's thinking, during all that time I had simply not been in existence, I'd been nothing, extinguished by Roithamer's thinking."

Walking offers a vision of a relatively early Bernhard. Of an artist whose major concerns—suicide, life as disease, the collapse of identity, the rottenness of Austria, the looming presence of death and madness—are already established, but whose style is still in the process of taking its final form. It has many of the satisfactions of Bernhard's later prose while at the same time suggesting other directions that Bernhard might have traveled.

Walking is a seminal work. It feels condensed and at times gnarled, as if Bernhard were trying to cram the thematic concerns of a longer novel into the smaller confines of the novella. In it, the narrator and his friend Oehler walk, discussing anything that comes to mind, but always circling back to their friend Karrer, who has recently gone irrevocably mad. The novella is a meditation on thinking—or, rather, on the impossibility of truly thinking. The majority of the narrative consists of Oehler talking and the narrator listening, sometimes responding. But Oehler's speech quotes Karrer and others, making the layering of the narrative both maddening and wonderfully complex. Four years later, after Bernhard loosened this structure slightly, covering similar themes but allowing them to develop over four times as many pages and with a more substantial narrative in play, he would produce his finest and most disturbing work, *Correction.*

Like many of Bernhard's works, *Walking* is unparagraphed. The structure is tripartite. The middle section recounts the events leading to Karrer's definitive breakdown. One is tempted to view this tripartite structure in Hegelian terms—as thesis, antithesis, synthesis—but if Bernhard employs such a model, it is fissured and cracked and ironized at the outset: the ideas of the sections bleed together and any synthesis is ultimately thwarted. The first and third sections in the novella are sufficiently similar that they might also be read as a single section split in halves by a trauma rising through it. It is perhaps analogous to Hegel's notion of the night of the world—the bloody head rising out of flux only to be swallowed up again—but twisted free of its philosophical significance and ultimate comforting contextualization: an eruption of a negativity through another negativity. In any case, Bernhard would not remain comfortable with the triad as a structural device (though he would use character triads); his later work moves away from structural triads toward dyads and monads, with longer works such as *Extinction* and *Correction* breaking into two long paragraphs, and shorter novels such as *Concrete* and *Wittgenstein's Nephew* consisting of a single sustained burst.

At the heart of the story lies madness. Karrer's "own daily discipline had been to school himself more and more in the most exciting, most tremendous, and most epoch-making thoughts with an ever greater determination, but only to the furthest possible point before absolute madness," but the difficulty is that "at any moment we can think too far." Thinking, in *Walking*, is like walking, and the characters think their ways along routes, with these routes leading sometimes over smooth ground and sometimes to the edge of an abyss. Suggests Oehler, "It is absolutely right to say, let's enter this thought, just as if we were to say, let's enter this haunted house." Indeed, language is viral, infecting through the ear the mind that takes it in: external words rewire internal thoughts. By entering into the thoughts of others we become possessed by their thoughts, potentially annihilating ourselves.

Walking is successful in its own terms even as it prepares for Bernhard's later novels, enriching and complicating our sense of one of the twentieth century's greatest writers.

Brian Evenson

WALK ING

TRANSLATED BY KENNETH J. NORTHCOTT

There is a constant tussle between all the possibilities of human thought and between all the possibilities of a human mind's sensitivity and between all the possibilities of a human character.

Whereas, before Karrer went mad, I used to go walking with Oehler only on Wednesday, now I go walking—now that Karrer has gone mad—with Oehler on Monday as well. Because Karrer used to go walking with me on Monday, you go walking with me on Monday as well, now that Karrer no longer goes walking with me on Monday, says Oehler, after Karrer had gone mad and had immediately gone into Steinhof. And without hesitation I said to Oehler, good, let's go walking on Monday as well. Whereas on Wednesday we always walk in one direction (in the eastern one), on Monday we go walking in the western direction, strikingly enough we walk far more quickly on Monday than on Wednesday, probably, I think, Oehler always walked more quickly with Karrer than he did with me, because on Wednesday he walks much more slowly and on Monday much more quickly. You see, says Oehler, it's a habit of mine to walk more quickly on Monday and more slowly on Wednesday because I always walked more quickly with Karrer (that is on Monday) than I did with you (on Wednesday). Because, after Karrer went mad, you now go walking with me not only on Wednesday but also on Monday, there is no need for me to alter

This translation of *Walking* first appeared in *Conjunctions*, vol. 32 (1999). I should like to acknowledge with gratitude the help and encouragement that I received from Brad Morrow, the editor of *Conjunctions*. –KJN my habit of going walking on Monday and on Wednesday, says Oehler, of course, because you go walking with me on Wednesday *and* Monday you have probably had to alter your habit and, actually, in what is probably for you an incredible fashion, says Oehler. But it is good, says Oehler, and he says it in an unmistakably didactic tone, and of the greatest importance for the organism, from time to time, and at not too great intervals, to alter a habit, and he says he is not thinking of just *altering*, but of a *radical alteration* of the habit. You are altering your habit, says Oehler, in that now you go walking with me not only on Wednesday but also on Monday and that now means walking alternately in one direction (in the Wednesday-) and in the other (in the Monday-) direction, while I am altering my habit in that until now I always went walking with you on Wednesday and with Karrer on Monday, but now I go with you on Monday and Wednesday, and thus also on Monday, and therefore on Wednesday in one (in the eastern) direction and on Monday in the other (in the western) direction. Besides which, I doubtless, and in the nature of things, walk differently with you than I did with Karrer, says Oehler, because with Karrer it was a question of a quite different person from you and therefore with Karrer it was a question of quite different walking (and thinking), says Oehler. The fact that I—after Karrer had gone mad and had gone into Steinhof, Oehler says, finally gone into Steinhof— had saved Oehler from the horror of having to go walking on his own on Monday, these were his own words, I would not have gone walking at all on Monday, says Oehler, for there is nothing more dreadful than having to go walking on one's own on Monday and having to walk on one's own is the most dreadful thing. I simply cannot imagine, says Oehler, that you would not go walking with me on Monday. And that I should have to go walking on my own on Monday is something that I cannot imagine. Whereas Oehler habitually wears his topcoat completely buttoned up, I leave my topcoat completely open. I think the reason for this is to be found in his persistent fear of getting chilled and catching a cold when leaving his topcoat open, whereas my reason is the persistent fear of suffocating if my topcoat is buttoned up. Thus Oehler is constantly afraid of getting cold whereas I am constantly afraid of suffocating. Whereas Oehler has on boots that reach up above his ankles, I wear ordinary shoes, for there is nothing I hate more than boots, just as Oehler hates nothing more than regular shoes. It is ill-bred (and stupid!) always to wear regular shoes, Oehler says again and again, while I say it's senseless to walk in such heavy boots. While Oehler has a wide-brimmed black hat, I have a narrow-brimmed gray one. If you could only get used to wearing a broad-brimmed hat like the one I wear, Oehler often says, whereas I often tell Oehler, if you could get used to wearing a narrow-brimmed hat like me. A narrow-brimmed hat doesn't suit your head, only a wide-brimmed one does, Oehler says to me, whereas I tell Oehler, only a narrow-brimmed hat suits your head, but not a wide-brimmed one like the one you have on. Whereas Oehler wears mittens—always the same mittens—thick, sturdy, woolen mittens that his sister knitted for him, I wear gloves, thin, though lined, pigskin gloves that my wife bought for me. One is only really warm in mittens, Oehler says over and over again, only in gloves, only in soft leather gloves like these, I say, can I move my hands as I do. Oehler wears black trousers with no cuffs, whereas I wear gray trousers with cuffs. But we never agree about our clothing and so there is no point in saying that Oehler should wear a narrow-brimmed hat, a pair of trousers with cuffs, topcoats that are not so tight as the one he has on, and so forth, or that I should wear mittens, heavy boots, and so forth, because we will not give up the clothing that we are wearing when we go walking and which we have been wearing for decades, no matter where we are going to, because this clothing, in the decades during which we have been wearing it, has become a fixed habit and so our fixed mode of dress. If we *hear* something, says Oehler, on Wednesday we check what we have heard and we check what we have heard until we have to say that what we have heard is not true, what we have heard is a lie. If we *see* something, we check what we see until we are forced to say that what we are looking at is horrible. Thus throughout our lives we never escape from what is horrible and what is untrue, the lie, says Oehler. If we *do* something, we think about what we are doing until we are forced to say that it is something nasty, something low, something outrageous, what we are doing is something terribly hopeless and that what we are doing is in the nature of things obviously false. Thus every day becomes hell for us whether we like it or not, and what we think will, if we think about it, if we have the requisite coolness of intellect and acuity of intellect, always become something nasty, something low and superfluous, which will depress us in the most shattering manner for the whole of our lives. For, everything that is thought is superfluous. Nature does not need thought, says Oehler, only human pride incessantly thinks into nature its thinking. What must *thoroughly* depress us is the fact that through this outrageous thinking into a nature that is, in the nature of things, fully immunized against this thinking, we enter into an even greater depression than that in which we already are. In the nature of things conditions become ever more unbearable through our thinking, says Oehler. If we think we are turning unbearable conditions into bearable ones, we have to realize quickly that we have not made (have not been able to make) unbearable circumstances bearable or even less bearable but only still more unbearable. And circumstances are the same as conditions, says Oehler, and it's the same with facts. The whole process of life is a process of deterioration in which everything—and this is the most cruel law—continually gets worse. If we look at a person, we are bound in a short space of time to say what a horrible, what an unbearable person. If we look at nature, we are bound to say, what a horrible, what an unbearable nature. If we look at something artificial—it doesn't matter what the artificiality is—we are bound to say in a short space of time what an unbearable artificiality. If we are out walking, we even say after the shortest space of time, what an unbearable walk, just as when we are running we say what an unbearable run, just as when we are standing still, what an unbearable standing still, just as when we are thinking what an unbearable process of thinking. If we meet someone, we think within the shortest space of time, what an unbearable meeting. If we go on a journey, we say to ourselves, after the shortest space of time, what an unbearable journey, what unbearable weather, we say, says Oehler, no matter what the weather is like, if we think about any sort of weather at all. If our intellect is keen, if our thinking is the most ruthless and the most lucid, says Oehler, we are bound after the shortest space of time to say of *everything* that it is unbearable and horrible. There is no doubt that the art lies in bearing what is unbearable and in not feeling that what is horrible is something horrible. Of course we have to label this art the most difficult of all. The art of existing against the facts, says Oehler, is the most difficult, the art that is the most difficult. To exist against the facts means existing against what is unbearable and horrible, says Oehler. If we do not constantly exist *against*, but only constantly *with* the facts, says Oehler, we shall go under in the shortest possible space of time. The fact is that our existence is an unbearable and horrible existence, if we exist *with* this fact, says Oehler, and not *against* this fact, then we shall go under in the most wretched and in the most usual manner, there should therefore be nothing more important to us than existing constantly, even if *in*, but also at the same time *against* the fact of an unbearable and horrible existence. The number of possibilities of existing *in* (*and with*) the fact of an unbearable and horrible existence, is the same as the number of existing against the unbearable and horrible existence and thus *in* (*and with*) and at the same time *against* the fact of an unbearable and horrible existence. It is always possible for people to exist *in* (*and with*) and, as a result, *in all* and *against* all facts, without existing against this fact and against all facts, just as it is always possible for them to exist in (and with) a fact and with all facts and against one and all facts and thus, above all, against the fact that existence is unbearable and horrible. It is always a question of intellectual indifference and intellectual acuity and of the ruthlessness of intellectual indifference and intellectual acuity, says Oehler. Most people, over ninety-eight percent, says Oehler, possess neither indifference of intellect nor acuity of intellect and do not even have the faculty of reason. The whole of history to date proves this without a doubt. Wherever we look, neither indifference of intellect, nor acuity of intellect, says Oehler, everything is a giant, a shatteringly long history without intellectual indifference and without acuity of intellect and so without the faculty of reason. If we look at history, it is above all its total lack of the faculty of reason that depresses us, to say nothing of intellectual indifference and acuity. To that extent it is no exaggeration to say that the whole of history is a history totally without reason, which makes it a *dead* history. We have, it is true, says Oehler, if we look at history, if we look into history, which a person like me is from time to time brave enough to do, a tremendous nature behind us, actually under us but in reality no history at all. History is a historical lie, is what I maintain, says Oehler. But let us return to the individual, says Oehler. To have the faculty of reason would mean nothing other than breaking off with history and first and foremost with one's own personal history. From one moment to the next simply to give up, accepting nothing more, that's what having the faculty of reason means, not accepting a person and not a thing, not a system and also, in the nature of things, not accepting a thought, just simply nothing more and then to commit suicide in this literally single revolutionary realization. But to think like this leads inevitably to sudden intellectual madness, says Oehler, as we know, and to what Karrer has had to pay for with sudden *total madness*. He, Oehler, did not believe that Karrer would ever be released from Steinhof, his madness is too fundamental for that, says Oehler. His own daily discipline had been to school himself more and more in the most exciting and in the most tremendous and most epoch-making thoughts with an ever greater determination, but only to the furthest possible point before absolute madness. If you go as far as Karrer, says Oehler, then you are suddenly decisively and absolutely mad and have, at one stroke, become useless. Go on thinking more and more and more and more with ever greater intensity and with an ever greater ruthlessness and with an ever greater fanaticism for finding out, says Oehler, but never for one moment think too far. At any moment we can think too far, says Oehler, simply go too far in our thoughts, says Oehler, and everything become valueless. I am now going to return once again, says Oehler, to what Karrer always came back to: that there is actually no faculty of reason in this world, or rather in what we call this world, because we have always called it this world, if we analyze what the faculty of reason is, we have to say that there simply is no faculty of reason—but Karrer had already analyzed that, says Oehler—that actually, as Karrer quite rightly said and the conclusion at which he finally arrived by his continued consideration of this incredibly fascinating subject, there is no faculty of reason, only an underfaculty of reason. The so-called human faculty of reason, says Oehler, is, as Karrer said, always a mere underfaculty of reason, even a subfaculty of reason. For if a faculty of reason were possible, says Oehler, then history would be possible, but history is not possible, because the faculty of reason is not possible and history does not arise from an underfaculty or a subfaculty of reason, a discovery of Karrer's, says Oehler. The fact of the underfaculty of reason, or of the so-called subfaculty of reason, says Oehler, does without doubt make possible the continued existence of nature through human beings. If I had a faculty of reason, says Oehler, if I had an unbroken faculty of reason, he says, I would long ago have committed suicide. What is to be understood from, or by, what I am saying, says Oehler, can be understood, what is not to be understood cannot be understood. Even if everything cannot be understood, everything is nevertheless unambiguous, says Oehler. What we call thinking has in reality nothing to do with the faculty of reason, says Oehler, Karrer is right about that when he says that we have no faculty of reason because we think, for to have a faculty of reason means not to think and so to have no thoughts. What we have is nothing but a substitute for a faculty of reason. A substitute for thought makes our existence possible. All the thinking that is done is only substitute thinking, because actual thinking is not possible, because there is no such thing as actual thinking, because nature excludes actual thinking, because it has to exclude actual thinking. You may think I'm mad, says Oehler, but actual, and that means real, thinking is completely excluded. But what we think is thinking we call thinking, just as what we consider to be walking we call walking, just as we say we are walking when we believe that we are walking and are actually walking, says Oehler. What I've just said has absolutely nothing to do with cause and effect, says Oehler. And there's no objection to saying *thinking*, where it's not a question of thinking, and there's no objection to saying *faculty of reason* where there's no possibility of its being a question of faculty of reason and there's no objection to saying *concepts* where they are not at issue. It is only by designating as actions and things actions and things that are in no way actions and things, because there is no way that they can be actions and things, that we get any farther, it is only in this way, says Oehler, that something is possible, indeed that anything is possible. Experience is a fact about which we know nothing and above all it is something which we cannot get to the root of, says Oehler. But on the other hand it is just as much a fact that we always act exactly or at least much more in concert with this fact, which is what I do (and recognize) when I say, these children, whom we see here in Klosterneuburgerstrasse, have been made because the faculty of reason was suspended, although we know that the concepts used in that statement, and as a result the words used in the statement, are completely false and thus we know that *everything* in the statement is false. Yet if we cling to our experience, which represents a zenith, and we can no longer sustain ourselves, then we no longer exist, says Oehler. Offhand, therefore I say, these children whom we see here in Klosterneuburgerstrasse were made because the faculty of reason was suspended. And it is only, because I do *not cling to experience*, that everything is possible. It is only possible in this way to utter a statement like: people simply walk along the street and make a child, or the statement: people have made a child because their faculty of reason is suspended. Oehler says, these people who make a child do not ask themselves anything, is a statement that is completely correct and at the same time completely false, like all statements. You have to know, says Oehler, that every statement that is uttered and thought and that exists is at the same time correct and at the same time false, if we are talking about proper statements. He now interrupts the conversation and says: In fact these people do not ask themselves anything when they make a child although they must know that to make a child and above all to make your own child means making a misfortune and thus making a child and thus making one's own child is nothing short of infamy. And when the child has been made, says Oehler, those who have made it allow the state to pay for it, this child they have made of their own free will. The state has to be responsible for these millions and millions of children who have been made completely of people's own free will, for the, as we know, completely superfluous children, who have contributed nothing but new, millionfold misfortune. The hysteria of history, says Oehler, overlooks the fact that in the case of all the children who are made it is a question of misfortune that has been made and a question of superfluity that has been made. We cannot spare the child makers the reproach that they have made their children without using their heads, and in the basest and lowest manner, although, as we know, they are not mindless. There is no greater catastrophe, says Oehler, than these children made mindlessly and whom the state, which has been betrayed by these children, has to pay for. Anyone who makes a child, says Oehler, deserves to be punished with the most extreme possible punishment and not to be subsidized. It is nothing but this completely false, so-called social, enthusiasm for subsidy by the state—which as we know is not social in the least, and of which it is said that it is nothing but the most distasteful anachronism in existence, and which is guilty of the fact that the crime of bringing a child into the world, which I call the greatest crime of all, says Oehler—that this crime, says Oehler, is not punished but is subsidized. The state should have the responsibility, Oehler now says, for punishing people who make children, but no, it subsidizes the crime. And the fact that all children who are made are made mindlessly, says Oehler, is a fact. And whatever is made mindlessly and above all whatever is made that is mindless should be punished. It should be the job of parliament and of parliaments to propose and carry out laws against the mindless making of children and to introduce and impose the supreme punishment, and everyone has his own supreme punishment, for the mindless making of children. After the introduction of such a law, says Oehler, the world would very quickly change to its own advantage. A state that subsidizes the making of children and not only the mindless making of children without using one's head, says Oehler, is a mindless state, certainly not a progressive one, says Oehler. The state that subsidizes the making of children has neither experience nor knowledge. Such a state is criminal, because it is quite consciously blind, such a state is not up-to-date, says Oehler, but we know that the up-to-date or, let's say, the so-called up-to-date state is simply not possible and thus this, our present, state cannot be in any shape or form a present-day state. Anyone who makes a child, says Oehler, knows that he is making a misfortune, he is making something that will be unhappy, because it has to be unhappy, something that is by nature totally catastrophic, in which again there is nothing else except what is by nature and which is bound to be totally catastrophic. He is making an endless misfortune, even if he makes only one child, says Oehler. It is a crime. We may never cease to say that anyone who makes a child, whether mindlessly or not, says Oehler, is committing a crime. At this moment, as we are walking along Klosterneuburgerstrasse, the situation is that there are so many, indeed hundreds of, children on Klosterneuburgerstrasse, and this prompts Oehler to continue his remarks about the making of children. To make a human being about whom we know that he does not want the life that has been made for him, says Oehler, for the fact that there is not a single human being who wants the life that has been made for him will certainly come out sooner or later, and before that person ceases to exist no matter who it is: to make such a person is really criminal. People in their baseness—disguised as helplessness—simply convince themselves that they want to have their lives, whereas in reality they never wished to have their lives, because they do not wish to perish because of the fact that nothing disgusts them more than their lives and, at root, nothing more than their irresponsible father, whether these fathers have already left their progeny or not, they do not want to perish because of this fact. All of these people convince themselves of this unbelievable lie. Millions convince themselves of this lie. They wish to have their lives, they say, and bear witness to it in public, day in day out, but the truth is that they do not want to have their lives. No one wants to have his life, says Oehler, everyone has come to terms with his life, but he does not want to have it, if he once has his life, says Oehler, he has to pretend to himself that his life is something, but in reality and in truth it is nothing but horrible to him. Life is not worth a single day, says Oehler, if you will only take the trouble to look at these hundreds of people here on this street, if you keep your eyes open where people are. If you walk along this street overflowing with children just once and keep your eyes open, says Oehler. So much helplessness and so much frightfulness and so much misery, says Oehler. The truth is no different from what I see here: frightful. I ask myself, says Oehler, how can so much helplessness and so much misfortune and so much misery be possible? That nature can create so much misfortune and so much palpable horror. That nature can be so ruthless toward its most helpless and pitiable creatures. This limitless capacity for suffering, says Oehler. This limitless capricious will to procreate and then to survive misfortune. In point of fact, right here in this street, this individual sickness, which runs into the thousands. Uncomprehending and helpless, says Oehler, you have to watch, day in day out, the making of masses of new and ever greater human misfortune, so much human ugliness, so much human atrocity, he says, every day, with unparalleled regularity and stupidity. You know yourself, says Oehler, just as I know myself, and all these people are also no different from us, but only unhappy and helpless and fundamentally lost. He, Oehler, to speak radically, stood for the gradual, total demise of the human race, if he had his way, no more children not a single one and thus no more human beings, not a single one. The world would slowly die out, says Oehler. Ever fewer human beings, finally no human beings at all, not a single human being more. But what he has just said, the earth gradually dying out and human beings growing fewer and fewer in the most natural way and finally dying out altogether, is only the raving of a mind that is already totally, and in the most total manner, working with the process of thinking and, in Oehler's own words, a *non*sense. Of course, an earth that was gradually dying out and finally one without human beings would probably be the most beautiful, says Oehler, after which he says, the thought is, of course *non*sense. But that doesn't alter the fact, says Oehler, that day in day out you have to stand by and see how more and more people are made with more and more inadequacy and with more and more misfortune, who have the same capacity for suffering and the same frightfulness and the same ugliness and the same detestableness as you yourself have, and who, as the years go by, have an even greater capacity for suffering and frightfulness and ugliness and detestableness. Karrer was of the same opinion, says Oehler. Oehler keeps repeating, *Karrer's view was the same* or *Karrer had a similar view* or *Karrer had a different* or *a contrary view* (*or opinion*). Karrer's statement always went: How do these people, who do not know how they get to such a point, and who have never been asked a question that affected them, how do all these people, with whom, if we think about it, we are bound again and again and with the greatest soundness of mind, to identify ourselves, throughout the course of their lives, no matter who they are, no matter what they are, and no matter where they are, how can they, I say, hurl themselves with ever more terrifying speed into, up into, and down into, their ultimate misfortune with all the horrible—that is human—means at their disposal? My whole life long, I have refused to make a child, said Karrer, Oehler says, to add a new human being over and above the person that I am, I who am sitting in the most horrible imaginable prison and whom science ruthlessly labels as human, I have refused to add a new human being to the person who is in the most horrible prison there is and to imprison a being who bears my name. If you walk along Klosterneuburgerstrasse, and especially if you walk along Klosterneuburgerstrasse with your eyes open, says Oehler, the making of children and everything connected with the making of children completely fades away from you. Then everything fades away from you, Oehler quotes Karrer as saying. I am struck by how often Oehler quotes Karrer without expressly drawing attention to the fact that he is quoting Karrer. Oehler frequently makes several statements that stem from Karrer and frequently thinks a thought that Karrer thought, I think, without expressly saying, what I am now saying comes from Karrer. *Fundamentally, everything that is said is a quotation* is also one of Karrer's statements, which occurs to me in this connection and which Oehler very often uses when it suits him. The constant use of the concept *human nature* and *nature* and in this connection *horrible* and *repugnant* and *dreadful* and *infinitely sad* and *frightful* and *disgusting* can all be traced back to Karrer. I think now that I went walking with Karrer on Klosterneuburgerstrasse for twenty years, says Oehler, like Karrer I grew up on Klosterneuburgerstrasse, and we both knew what it means to have grown up on Klosterneuburgerstrasse, this knowledge has underlain all our actions and all our thinking and, especially, the whole time we were walking together. Karrer's pronunciation was the clearest, Karrer's thought the most correct, Karrer's character the most irreproachable, says Oehler. But recently I had already detected signs of fatigue in his person, above all in his mind, on the other hand his mind was unbelievably active, in a way I had never noticed before. On the one hand Karrer's body, which had suddenly grown old, says Oehler, on the other, Karrer's mind, which was capable of incredible intellectual acuity. His sudden physical decrepitude on the one hand, says Oehler, the sudden weirdness and outrageousness of the thoughts in his head on the other. Whereas Karrer's body, especially in the past year, could very often be seen as a body that had already declined and was in the process of disintegrating, says Oehler, the capacity of his mind was at the same time, in its outrageousness, truly terrifying to me. I suddenly had to consider what sorts of outrageousness this mind of Karrer's was capable of, says Oehler, on the other hand how decrepit this body of Karrer's is, a body that is not yet really old. Doubtless, says Oehler, Karrer went mad when he was at the height of his thinking. This is an observation that science can always make in the case of people like Karrer. That they suddenly, at the height of their thinking, and thus at the height of their intellectual capacity, become mad. There is a moment, says Oehler, at which madness *enters*. It is a single moment in which the person affected *is suddenly mad*. Again, Oehler says: in Karrer's case it is a question of a total, final madness. There's no point in thinking that Karrer will come out of Steinhof again as he did eight years ago. We shall probably never see Karrer again, says Oehler. There is every sign, says Oehler, that Karrer will stay in Steinhof and not come out of Steinhof again. The depression caused by a visit to Karrer in Steinhof would probably be so violent, says Oehler, especially for his mind and as a result, in the nature of things, for his thinking, that such a visit would have the most devastating effect, so that there is no point in thinking about a visit to Karrer in Steinhof. Not even if we were to go together to visit Karrer, says Oehler. If I go alone to see Karrer, it will be the ruin of me for weeks, if not for months, if not forever, says Oehler. Even if you visit Karrer, says Oehler to me, it will be the ruin of you. And if we go together, a visit of that sort would have the same effect on both of us. To visit a person in the condition that Karrer finds himself at the moment would be nonsense, because visiting a person who is totally and finally mad makes no sense. Quite apart from the fact, says Oehler, that every visit to Steinhof has depressed me, visiting a lunatic asylum requires the greatest effort, says Oehler, if the visitor is not a fool without feeling or the capacity to think. It makes me feel ill even to approach Steinhof, let alone go inside. The world outside lunatic asylums is scarcely to be borne, he says. If we see hundreds and thousands of people, of whom, with the best will in the world and with the greatest self-abnegation, we cannot say that we are still dealing with human beings, he says. If we always see that things are much worse in lunatic asylums than we imagined they were before we visited a lunatic asylum. Then, when we are in Steinhof, says Oehler, we recognize that the unbearableness of life outside lunatic asylums—which we have always separated from the life and existence and existence from life and the existence and existing inside lunatic asylums—*outside* lunatic asylums is really laughable compared with the insupportability *in* lunatic asylums. If we are qualified to compare, says Oehler, and to declare ourselves satisfied with the justness of the concepts of inside and outside, that is, inside and outside lunatic asylums, and with the justness of the concepts of the so-called intact as distinct from the concepts of the so-called nonintact world. If we have to tell ourselves that it is only a question of the brutality of a moment to go to Steinhof. And if we know that this moment can be any moment. If we know that every moment can be the one when we cross the border into Steinhof. If you had said to Karrer three weeks ago that he would be in Steinhof today, says Oehler, Karrer would have expressed doubt, even if he had taken into consideration the possibility that at any moment he might be back in Steinhof. Here on this very spot, I said to Karrer, says Oehler, and he stops walking: if it is possible to control the moment that no one has yet controlled, the moment of the final crossing of the border into Steinhof, and that is, into final madness, without being able to finish the unfinished statement, says Oehler, Karrer said at that time, he did not understand what was doubtless an unfinished statement, but that he knew what was meant by this unfinished statement. Even Karrer did not succeed where no one has yet succeeded, says Oehler, in knowing the moment when the border to Steinhof is to be crossed and thus the moment the border into final madness is to be crossed. When we do something, we may not think about why we are doing what we are doing, says Oehler, for then it would suddenly be totally impossible for us to do anything. We may not make what we are doing the object of our thought, for then we would first be the victims of *mortal doubt* and, finally, of *mortal despair*. Just as we may not think about what is going on around us and what has gone on and what will go on, if we do not have the strength to break off our thinking about what happens around us and what has happened and what will happen, that is about the past, the present and the future at precisely the moment when this thinking becomes fatal for us. The art of thinking about things consists in the art, says Oehler, of stopping thinking before the fatal moment. However, we can, quite consciously, drag out this fatal moment, says Oehler, for a longer or a shorter time, according to circumstances. But the important thing is for us to know when the fatal moment is. But no one knows when the fatal moment is, says Oehler, the question is, is it possible that the fatal moment has not yet come and will always not yet come? But we cannot rely on this. We may never think, says Oehler, how and why we are doing what we are doing, for then we would be condemned, even if not instantaneously, but instantaneously to whatever degree of awareness we have reached regarding that question, to total inactivity and to complete immobility. For the clearest thought, that which is the deepest and, at the same time, the most transparent, is the most complete inactivity and the most complete immobility, says Oehler. We may not think about why we are walking, says Oehler, for then it would soon be impossible for us to walk, and then, to take things to their logical conclusion. Everything soon becomes impossible, just as when we are thinking why we may not think, why we are walking and so on, just as we may not think how we are walking, how we are not walking, that is standing still, just as we may not think how we, when we are not walking and standing still, are thinking and so on. We may not ask ourselves: why are we walking? as others who may (and can) ask themselves at will why they are walking. The others, says Oehler, may (and can) ask themselves anything, we may not ask ourselves anything. In the same way, if it is a question of objects, we may also not ask ourselves, just as if it is not a question of objects (the opposite of objects). What we see we think, and, as a result, do not see it, says Oehler, whereas others have no problem in seeing what they are seeing because they do not think what they see. What we call perception is really stasis, immobility, as far as we are concerned, nothing. Nothing. What has happened is thought, not seen, says Oehler. Thus quite naturally when we see, we see nothing, we think everything at the same time. Suddenly Oehler says, if we visited Karrer in Steinhof, we would be just as shocked as we were eight years ago, but now Karrer's madness is not only much worse than his madness of eight years ago, now it is final and if we think how shocked we were eight years ago during our visit to Karrer it would be senseless to think for a moment of visiting Karrer now that Karrer's condition is a dreadful one. Karrer is probably not allowed to receive visitors, says Oehler. Karrer is in Pavilion VII, in the one that is most dreaded. What horrible prisons these the most pitiable of all creatures are locked up in, says Oehler. Nothing but filth and stench. Everything rusted and decayed. We hear the most unbelievable things, we see the most unbelievable things. Oehler says: Karrer's world is his own to the same extent that it is ours. I could just as well be walking here with Karrer along Klosterneuburgerstrasse and be talking with Karrer about *you*, if you and not Karrer were in Steinhof at the moment, or if it were the case that they had sent me to Steinhof and confined me there and you were out walking with Karrer through Klosterneuburgerstrasse and talking about me. We are not certain whether we ourselves will not, the very next moment, be in the same situation as the person we are talking about and who is the object of our thought. *I* could just as well have gone mad in Rustenschacher's store, says Oehler, if I had gone into Rustenschacher's store that day in the same condition as Karrer to engage in the argument with Rustenschacher in which Karrer had been engaged and if I, like Karrer, had not accepted the consequences that followed from the argument in Rustenschacher's store and was now in Steinhof. But in fact it is impossible that I would have acted like Karrer, says Oehler, because I am not Karrer, *I would have acted like myself*, just as *you would have acted like yourself* and not like Karrer, and even if I had entered Rustenschacher's store, like Karrer, to begin an argument with Rustenschacher and his nephew, I would have carried on the argument in a quite different manner and of course everything would have turned out differently from what it did between Karrer and Rustenschacher and Rustenschacher's nephew. The argument would have been a different argument, it simply wouldn't have come to an argument, for if I had been in Karrer's position, I would have carried on the argument quite differently and probably not carried it on at all, says Oehler. A set of several fatal circumstances, which are of themselves not fatal at all and only become fatal when they coincide, leads to a misfortune like the one that befell Karrer in Rustenschacher's store, says Oehler. Then we are standing there because we had witnessed it all and react as though we had been insulted. It is unthinkable to me that, if I had been Karrer, I would have gone into Rustenschacher's store that afternoon, but Karrer's intensity that afternoon was a greater intensity and I followed Karrer into Rustenschacher's store. But to ask *why* I followed Karrer into Rustenschacher's store that afternoon is senseless. Then let's say that what we have here is a *tragedy*, says Oehler. We judge an unexpected happening, like the occurrence in Rustenschacher's store, as irrevocable and calculated where there is no justification for the concepts irrevocable and calculated. For nothing is irrevocable and nothing is calculated, but a lot, and often what is the most dreadful, simply happens. I can now say that I am astonished at my passivity in Rustenschacher's store, my unbelievable silence, the fact that I stood by and fundamentally reacted to *nothing*, that I did fear something without knowing (or suspecting) what I feared, but that in the face of such a fear and thus in the face of Karrer's condition, I did nothing. We say that circumstances bring about a certain condition in people. If that is true, then circumstances brought about a condition in Karrer in which he suddenly went finally mad in Rustenschacher's store. I must say, says Oehler, that it was a question of fear of ceasing to be senselessly patient. We observe a person in a desperate situation, the concept of a desperate situation is clear to us, but we do nothing about the desperate condition of the person, because we can do nothing about the desperate condition of the person, because in the truest sense of the word we are powerless in the face of a person's desperate condition, although we do not have to be powerless in the face of such a person and his desperate condition, and this is something we have to admit, says Oehler. We are suddenly conscious of the hopelessness of a desperate nature, but by then it is too late. It is not Rustenschacher and his nephew who are guilty, says Oehler. Those two behaved as they had to behave, obviously so as not to be sacrificed to Karrer. The circumstance did not, however, arise in a very short space of time, says Oehler, these circumstances always, and in every case, arise as the result of a process that has lasted a long time. The circumstances that led to Karrer's madness in Rustenschacher's store and to Karrer's argument with Rustenschacher and his nephew did not arise on that day nor on that afternoon and not just in the preceding twenty-four or forty-eight hours. We always look for everything in the immediate proximity, that is a mistake. If only we did not always look for everything in the immediate proximity, says Oehler, looking in the immediate proximity reveals nothing but incompetence. One should, in every case, go back *over everything*, says Oehler, even if it is in the depths of the past and scarcely ascertainable and discernible any longer. Of course the most nonsensical thing, says Oehler, is to ask oneself why one went into Rustenschacher's store with Karrer, to say nothing of reproaching oneself for doing so. He was obliged, he says, to repeat that in this case everything, and at the same time nothing, indicated that Karrer would suddenly go mad. If we may not ask ourselves the simplest of questions, then we may not ask ourselves a question like the question why Karrer went into Rustenschacher's store in the first place, for there was absolutely no need to do so if you disregard the fact that, possibly, Karrer's sudden fatigue after our walk to Albersbachstrasse and back again was actually a reason, nor may we ask why I followed Karrer into Rustenschacher's store. But as we do not ask, we may not, by the same token, say that everything was a foregone conclusion, was self-evident. Suddenly, at this moment, what had until then, been possible, would now be impossible, says Oehler. On the other hand what is, is self-evident. What he sees while we are walking, he sees through, and for this reason he does not observe at all, for anything that can be seen through (completely) cannot be observed. Karrer also made this same observation, says Oehler. If we see through something, we have to say that we do not see that thing. On the other hand no one else sees the thing, for anyone who does not see through a thing does not see the thing either. Karrer was of the same opinion. The question, why do I get up in the morning? can (must) be absolutely fatal if it is asked in such a way as to be really asked and if it is taken to a conclusion or has to be taken to a conclusion. Like the question, why do I go to bed at night? Like the question, why do I eat? Why do I dress? Why does everything (or a great deal or a very little) connect me to some people and nothing at all to others? If the question is taken to a logical conclusion, which means that the person who asks a question, which he takes to its logical conclusion *because* he takes it to a conclusion or because he has to take it to a conclusion, also takes it to a conclusion, then the question is answered once and for all, and then the person who asked the question does not exist any longer. If we say that this person is dead from the moment when he answers his own question, we make things too simple, says Oehler. On the other hand, we can find no better way of expressing it than by saying that the person who asked the question is dead. Since we cannot name everything and so cannot think *absolutely*, we exist and there is an existence outside of ourselves, says Oehler. If we have come as far as we have come (in thought), says Oehler, we must take the consequences and we must abandon these (or the) thoughts that have (or has) made it possible for us to come this far. Karrer exercised this faculty with a virtuosity which, according to Karrer, could only be called mental agility, says Oehler. If we suppose that I, and not Karrer, were in Steinhof now, says Oehler, and you were talking to me here, the thought is nonsensical, says Oehler. The chemist Hollensteiner's suicide had a catastrophic effect upon Karrer, says Oehler, it had to have the effect upon Karrer that it did, rendering chaotic, in the most devastating manner, Karrer's completely unprotected mental state in the most fatal manner. Hollensteiner, who had been a friend of Karrer's in his youth, had, as will be recalled, committed suicide just at the moment when the so-called Ministry of Education withdrew funds vital to his Institute of Chemistry. The state withdraws vital funds from the most extraordinary minds, says Oehler, and it is precisely because of this that the extraordinary and the most extraordinary minds commit suicide, and Hollensteiner was one of these most extraordinary minds. I, says Oehler, could not begin to list the number of extraordinary and most extraordinary minds—all of them young and brilliant minds—who have committed suicide because the state, in whatever form, had withdrawn vital funds from them, and there is no doubt, in my mind, that in Hollensteiner's case we are talking about a genius. At the very moment that was most vital to Hollensteiner's institute, and so to Hollensteiner himself, the state withdrew the funds from him (and thus from his institute). Hollensteiner, who had, in his own day, made a great name for himself in chemistry, which is today such an important area of expertise, at a time when no one in this, his own country, had heard of him, even today, if you ask, no one knows the name Hollensteiner, says Oehler, we mention a completely extraordinary man's name, says Oehler, and we discover that no one knows the name, especially not those who ought to know the name: this is always our experience, the people who ought to know the name of their most extraordinary scientist do not know the name or else they do not want to know the name. In this case, the chemists do not even know Hollensteiner's name, or else they do not want to know the name Hollensteiner, and so Hollensteiner was driven to suicide, just like all extraordinary minds in this country. Whereas in Germany the name Hollensteiner was one of the most respected among chemists and still is today, here in Austria Hollensteiner has been completely blotted out, in this country, says Oehler, the extraordinary has always, and in all ages, been blotted out, blotted out until it committed suicide. If an Austrian mind is extraordinary, says Oehler, we do not need to wait for him to commit suicide, it is only a question of time and the state counts on it. Hollensteiner had so many offers, says Oehler, none of which he accepted, however. In Basel they would have welcomed Hollensteiner with open arms, in Warsaw, in Copenhagen, in Oxford, in America. But Hollensteiner didn't even go to Göttingen, where they would have given Hollensteiner all the funds he wanted, because he couldn't go to Göttingen, a person like Hollensteiner is incapable of going to Göttingen, of going to Germany at all; before a person like that would go to Germany he would rather commit suicide first. And at the very moment when he depends, in the most distressing manner, on the help of the state, he kills himself, which means that the state kills him. Genius is abandoned and driven to suicide. A scientist, says Oehler, is in a sad state in Austria and sooner or later, but especially at the moment when it appears to be most senseless, he has to perish because of the stupidity of the world around him and that means because of the stupidity of the state. We have an extraordinary scientist and ignore him, no one is attacked more basely than the extraordinary man, and genius goes to the dogs because in this state it has to go to the dogs. If only an eminent authority like Hollensteiner had the strength and, to as great an extent, the tendency toward self-denial so as to give up Austria, and that means Vienna, and go to Marburg or Göttingen, to give only two examples that apply to Hollensteiner, and could there, in Marburg or in Göttingen, continue the scientific work that it has become impossible for him to continue in Vienna, says Oehler, but a man like Hollensteiner was not in a position to go to Marburg or to Göttingen, Hollensteiner was precisely the sort of person who was unable to go to Germany. But it was also impossible for Hollensteiner to go to America, as we see, for then Hollensteiner, who was unable to go to Germany because the country made him feel uncomfortable and was intensely repugnant to him, would indeed have gone to America. Very, very few people have the strength to abandon their dislike of the country that is fundamentally ready to accept them with open arms and unparalleled goodwill and to go to that country. They would rather commit suicide in their own country because ultimately their love of their own country, or rather their love of their own, the Austrian, landscape, is greater than the strengths to endure their own science in another country. As far as Hollensteiner is concerned, says Oehler, we have an example of how the state treats an unusually clear and important mind. For years Hollensteiner begged for the funds that he needed for his own research, says Oehler, for years Hollensteiner demeaned himself in the face of a bureaucracy that is the most repugnant in the whole world, in order to get his funds, for years Hollensteiner tried what hundreds of extraordinary and brilliant people have tried. To realize an important, and not only for Austria but, without a shadow of doubt, for the whole of mankind, undertaking of a scientific nature with the aid of state funds. But he had to admit that in Austria no one can realize anything with the help of state funds, least of all something extraordinary, significant, epoch-making. The state, to whom a nature like Hollensteiner's turns in the depths of despair, has no time for a nature like Hollensteiner's. Thus a nature like Hollensteiner's must recognize that it lives in a state, and we must say this about the state without hesitation and with the greatest ruthlessness, that hates the extraordinary and hates nothing more than the extraordinary. For it is clear that, in this state, only what is stupid, impoverished, and dilettante is protected and constantly promoted and that, in this state, funds are only invested in what is incompetent and superfluous. We see hundreds of examples of this every day. And this state claims to be a civilized state and demands that it be described as such on every occasion. Let's not fool ourselves, says Oehler, this state has nothing to do with a civilized state and we shall never tire of saying so continually and without cease and on every occasion even if we are faced with the greatest difficulties because of our ceaseless observation, as a repetition of the same thing over and over again, that this is a state where lack of feeling and sense is boundless. It was Hollensteiner's misfortune to be tied by all his senses to this country, not to this state, you understand, but to this country. And we know what it means, says Oehler, to love a country like ours with all of one's senses in contrast to a state that does everything it can to destroy you instead of coming to your aid. Hollensteiner's suicide is one suicide among many, every year we are made aware of the fact that many people whom we value and who have had talent and genius and who were extraordinary or most extraordinary have committed suicide, for we are constantly going to cemeteries, says Oehler, to the funerals of people who, despairing of the state, have committed suicide, who, if we stop to think, have thrown themselves out of windows or hanged themselves or shot themselves because they felt that they had been abandoned by our state. The only reason we go to cemeteries, says Oehler, is to inter a genius who has been ruined by the state and driven to his death, that is the truth. If we strike a balance between the beauty of the country and the baseness of the state, says Oehler, we arrive at suicide. As far as Hollensteiner was concerned, it became clear that his suicide was bound to distress Karrer, after all, the two had had an unbelievable relationship as friends. Only I always thought that Hollensteiner had the strength to go to Germany, to Göttingen, where he would have had everything at his disposal, says Oehler: the fact that he did not have this strength was the cause of his death. It would also have been of no use to have tried even more intensely to persuade him to go to Göttingen at any price, Karrer said, says Oehler. A nature that was not quite as sensitive as Hollensteiner's would of course have had the strength to go to Göttingen, to go anywhere at all, simply to go where all the necessary funds for his scientific purposes would be at his disposal, says Oehler. But for a nature like Hollensteiner's it is, of course, utterly impossible to settle down in an environment, especially for scientific purposes and in any scientific discipline, that is unbearable to that nature. And it would be senseless, says Oehler, to leave a country that you love but in which you are bound, as we can see, gradually to perish in a morass of indifference and stupidity, and go to a country where you will never get over the depression that that country breeds in you, never get out of a state of mind that must be equally destructive: then it would be better to commit suicide in the country you love, if only out of force of habit, says Oehler, rather than in the country that, not to mince words, you hate. People like Hollensteiner are admittedly the most difficult, says Oehler, and it is not easy to keep in contact with them because these people are constantly giving offense—a characteristic of extraordinary people, their most outstanding characteristic, giving offense—but on the other hand there is no greater pleasure than being in contact with such extremely difficult people. We must leave no stone unturned, says Oehler, and we must always, quite consciously, set the highest value on keeping in contact with these extremely difficult people, with the extraordinary and the most extraordinary, because this is the only contact that has any real value. All other contacts are worthless, says Oehler, they are necessary but worthless. It is a shame, says Oehler, that I didn't meet Hollensteiner a lot earlier, but a remarkable caution toward this person, whom I always admired, did not permit me to make closer contact with Hollensteiner for at least twenty years after I had first set eyes on Hollensteiner, and even then our contact was not the intense contact that I would have wished for. People like Hollensteiner, says Oehler, do not allow you to approach them, they attract you and then at the crucial moment reject you. We think we have a close relationship with these people whereas in reality we can never establish a close relationship with people like Hollensteiner. In fact, we are captivated by such people as Hollensteiner without exactly knowing the reason why. On the one hand it is not, in fact, the person, on the other it is not their science, for we do not understand either of them. It is something of which we cannot say what it is and *because of that* it has the greatest effect upon us. For, says Oehler, you have to have gone to elementary school, to secondary school, and to the university with a man like Hollensteiner, as Karrer did, to know what he is. A person like me doesn't know. We comment, with really terrifying helplessness, upon a matter or a case or simply just a misfortune or just simply Hollensteiner's misfortune. I talked to Karrer about this at precisely the place where we are now standing, a few hours after we had attended Hollensteiner's funeral. Just in Döblingen cemetery itself, says Oehler, where we buried Hollensteiner and, in the nature of things, buried him in the simplest way. He wanted to have a very simple funeral, says Oehler, he had once indicated to Karrer, actually very early on when he was only twenty-one, he had indicated that he wanted a very simple funeral and in Döblingen cemetery. Just in Döblingen cemetery itself, says Oehler, there are so many extraordinary people buried, all of whom were destroyed by the state, who perished as a result of the brutality of the bureaucracy and the stupidity of the masses. We comment upon a thing, a case, or simply a misfortune and wonder how this misfortune could have arisen. How was this misfortune *possible?* We deliberately avoid talking about a so-called *human tragedy*. We have a single individual in front of us, and we have to tell ourselves that this individual has perished at the hands of the state and, vice versa, that the state has perished at the hands of this individual. It is not easy to say that it's a question of a misfortune, says Oehler, of this individual's misfortune, or the state's misfortune. It makes no sense to tell ourselves, now, that Hollensteiner could be in Göttingen (or Marburg) now, because Hollensteiner is not in Göttingen and is not in Marburg. Hollensteiner no longer exists. We buried Hollensteiner in Döblingen cemetery. As far as Hollensteiner is concerned we are left behind with our absolute helplessness (of thought). What we do is to exhaust ourselves meditating about insoluble facts, among which we do not understand the process of thought, though we call it thought, says Oehler. We become aware once more of our unease when we occupy ourselves with Hollensteiner, with Hollensteiner's suicide and with Karrer's madness, which I think is directly connected to Hollensteiner's suicide. We even misuse a subject like that of Hollensteiner in relation to Karrer, to bring ourselves satisfaction. A strange ruthlessness, which is not recognizable as ruthlessness, dominates a man like Hollensteiner, says Oehler, and we are inevitably captivated by this ruthlessness if we recognize that it is an incredibly shrewd emotional state, which we could also call a state of mind. Anyone who knew Hollensteiner had to ask himself now and again where Hollensteiner's way of acting would lead. Today we can see quite clearly where Hollensteiner's way of acting has led. Hollensteiner and Karrer together represent the two most unusual people I have known, says Oehler. There is no doubt that the fact that Hollensteiner hanged himself in his institute is demonstrative in character, says Oehler. The shock of Hollensteiner's suicide was, however, like all shocks about suicides, very very short-lived. Once the suicide is buried, his suicide and he himself are forgotten. No one thinks about it any more and the shock turns out to be hypocritical. Between Hollensteiner's suicide and Hollensteiner's funeral a lot was said about saving the Institute of Chemistry, says Oehler, people saying that the funds that had been denied to Hollensteiner would be placed at the disposal of his successor, as if there were one! cries Oehler, the newspapers carried reports that the ministry would undertake a so-called extensive redevelopment of Hollensteiner's institute, at the funeral, people were even talking about the state's making good what it had until then neglected in the Institute for Chemistry, but today, a few weeks later, says Oehler, that's all as good as forgotten. Hollensteiner demonstrates by hanging himself in his own institute the serious plight of the whole domestic scientific community, says Oehler, and the world, and thus the people around Hollensteiner, feigns shock and goes to Hollensteiner's funeral, and the moment Hollensteiner is buried they forget everything connected with Hollensteiner. Today nobody talks about Hollensteiner any more and nobody talks about his Institute of Chemistry, and nobody thinks of changing the situation that led to Hollensteiner's suicide. And then someone else commits suicide, says Oehler, and another, and the process is repeated. Slowly but surely all intellectual activity in this country is extinguished, says Oehler. And what we observe in

Hollensteiner's field can be seen in every field, says Oehler. Until now we have always asked ourselves whether a country, a state, can afford to allow its intellectual treasure to deteriorate in such a really shabby way, says Oehler, but nobody asks the question any longer. Karrer spoke about Hollensteiner as a perfect example of a human being who could not be helped because he was extraordinary, unusual. Karrer explained the concept of the eccentric in connection with Hollensteiner with complete clarity, says Oehler. If there had been a less fundamental, a distanced, relationship between him, Karrer, and Hollensteiner, Karrer told Oehler, he, Karrer, would have made Hollensteiner the subject of a paper entitled *The Relationship between Persons and Characters Like Hollensteiner, as a Chemist, to the State, Which is Gradually and in the Most Consistent Manner Destroying and Killing Them*. In fact, there are in existence a number of Karrer's remarks about Hollensteiner, says Oehler, hundreds of slips of paper, just as there are about you, says Oehler to me, there are in existence hundreds of Karrer's slips of paper just as there are about me. It is obvious that these slips of paper written by Karrer should not be allowed to disappear, but it is difficult to get at these notes of Karrer's, if we want to secure Karrer's writings, we have to apply to Karrer's sister, but she doesn't want to hear anything more about Karrer's thoughts. He, Oehler, thinks that Karrer's sister may already have destroyed Karrer's writings, for as we see over and over again stupid relatives act quickly, as, for example, the sisters or wives or brothers and nephews of dead thinkers, or ones who have gone finally mad, even when it is a case of brilliant characters, as in the case of Karrer, they don't even wait for the actual moment of death or the final madness of the hated object, says Oehler, but acting as their relatives destroy, that is burn, the writings that irritate them for the most part before the final death or the final confinement of their hated thinker. Just as Hollensteiner's sister destroyed everything that Hollensteiner wrote, immediately after Hollensteiner's suicide. It would be a mistake to assume that Hollensteiner's sister would have taken Hollensteiner's part, says Oehler, on the contrary Hollensteiner's sister was ashamed of Hollensteiner and had taken the state's part, the part, that is, of baseness and stupidity. When Karrer went to see her, she threw him out, says Oehler, that is to say she didn't even let Karrer into her house. And to his question about Hollensteiner's writings she replied that Hollensteiner's writings no longer existed, she had burned Hollensteiner's writings because they appeared to her to be the writings of a madman. The fact is, says Oehler, that the world lost tremendous thoughts in Hollensteiner's writings, philosophy lost tremendous philosophical thoughts, science lost tremendous scientific thoughts. For Hollensteiner had been a continuous, thinking, scientific mind, says Oehler, who constantly put his continuous scientific thought onto paper. In fact, in Hollensteiner's case, we were dealing not only with a scientist but also with a philosopher, in Hollensteiner the scientist and the philosopher were able to fuse into one single, clear intellect, says Oehler. Thus, when you talk of Hollensteiner, you can speak of a scientist who was basically really a philosopher, just as you can speak of a philosopher who was basically really a scientist. Hollensteiner's science was basically philosophy, Hollensteiner's philosophy basically science, says Oehler. Otherwise we are always forced to say, here we have a scientist but (regrettably) not a philosopher, or here we have a philosopher but (regrettably) not a scientist. This is not the case in our judgment of Hollensteiner. It is a very Austrian characteristic, as we know, says Oehler. If we get involved with Hollensteiner, says Oehler, we get involved with a philosopher and a scientist at the same time, even if it were totally false to say that Hollensteiner was a philosophizing scientist and so on. He was a totally scientific philosopher. If we are talking about a person, as we are at the moment about Hollensteiner (and if we are talking about Hollensteiner, then basically about Karrer, but very often basically about Hollensteiner and so on), we are nevertheless speaking all the time about a result. We are mathematicians, says Oehler, or at least we are always trying to be mathematicians. When we think, it is less a case of philosophy, says Oehler, more one of mathematics. Everything is a tremendous calculation, if we have set it up from the outset in an unbroken line, *a very simple* calculation. But we are not always in the position of keeping everything that we have calculated intact within our head, and we break off what we are thinking and are satisfied with what we see, and are not surprised for long that we rest content with what we see, with millions upon millions of images that lie on, or under, one another and constantly merge and displace each other. Again, we can say that what appears extraordinary to a person like me, what is in fact extraordinary to me, *because* it is extraordinary, says Oehler, means nothing to the state. For Hollensteiner meant nothing to the state because he meant nothing to the masses, but we shall not get any further with this thought, says Oehler. And whereas the state and whereas society and whereas the masses do everything to get rid of thought, *we* oppose this development with all the means at our disposal, although we ourselves believe most of the time in the senselessness of thinking, because we know that thinking is total senselessness, because, on the other hand, we know that without the senselessness of thinking *we* do not exist or are nothing. We then cling to the effortlessness with which the masses dare to exist, although they deny this effortlessness in every statement that they make, says Oehler, but, in the nature of things, we do not, of course, succeed in being really effortless in the effortlessness of the masses. We can, however, do nothing less than cling to this misconception from time to time, subject ourselves to the misconception, and that means all possible misconceptions, and exist in nothing but misconception. For strictly speaking, says Oehler, everything is misconceived. But we exist within this fact because there is no way that we can exist outside this fact, at least not all the time. Existence is misconception, says Oehler. This is something we have to come to terms with early enough, so that we have a basis upon which we can exist, says Oehler. Thus misconception is the only real basis. But we are not always obliged to think of this basis as a principle, we must not do that, says Oehler, we cannot do that. We can only say yes, over and over again, to what we should unconditionally say no to, do you understand, says Oehler, that is the fact. Thus Karrer's madness was causally connected with Hollensteiner's suicide, which of itself had nothing to do with madness. Behavior like Hollensteiner's was bound to do damage to a nature like Karrer's if we consider Hollensteiner's relationship to Karrer and vice versa, in the way in which Hollensteiner's suicide harmed Karrer's nature, says Oehler. Karrer had on many occasions, he went on, spoken to Oehler of the possibility of Hollensteiner's committing suicide. But he was talking about a suicide that would come *from within*, not of one that would *be caused externally*, says Oehler, if we disregard the fact that inner and outer are identical for natures like Hollensteiner and Karrer. For, and these are Karrer's words, says Oehler, the possibility that Hollensteiner would commit suicide from an inner cause always existed, but then with the extension of Hollensteiner's institute and with Hollensteiner's obvious successes in his scientific work, simultaneously with the ignoring and the torpedoing of these scientific successes of Hollensteiner's by the world around him, the possibility existed that he would commit suicide from *an external cause*. Whereas, however, it is characteristic and typical of Hollensteiner, says Oehler, that he did finally commit suicide, as we now know, and what we could not know up to the moment that Hollensteiner committed suicide is that it is also typical of Karrer that he did not commit suicide after Hollensteiner had committed suicide but that he, Karrer, went mad. However, what is frightful, says Oehler, is the thought that a person like Karrer, because he has gone mad and, as I believe, has actually gone finally mad, because he has gone finally mad he has fallen into the hands of people like Scherrer. On the previous Saturday, Oehler made several statements regarding Karrer to Scherrer which, according to Scherrer, says Oehler, were of importance for him, Scherrer, in connection with Karrer's treatment, he, Oehler, did not believe that what he had told Scherrer on Saturday, especially about the incident that was crucial for Karrer's madness, the incident in Rustenschacher's men's store, that the very thing that Oehler had told Scherrer about what he had noticed in Rustenschacher's store, shortly before Karrer went mad, still made sense. For Scherrer's scientific work *it did*, for Karrer *it did not*. For the fact that Scherrer now knows what I noticed in Rustenschacher's store before Karrer went mad in Rustenschacher's store makes no difference to Karrer's madness. What happened in Rustenschacher's store, says Oehler, was only the factor that triggered Karrer's final madness, nothing more. For example, it would have been much more important, says Oehler, if Scherrer had concerned himself with the relationship of Karrer and Hollensteiner, but Scherrer did not want to hear anything from Oehler about this relationship, Karrer's relationship to Hollensteiner was not of the slightest interest to Scherrer, says Oehler. I tried several times to direct Scherrer's attention to this relationship, to make him aware of this really important relationship and of the really important events that took place within this year- and decades-long connection between Karrer and Hollensteiner, but Scherrer did not go into it, says Oehler, but, as is the way with these people, these totally unphilosophical and, for that reason, useless psychiatric doctors, he continued to nag away at the happenings in Rustenschacher's store, which are, in my opinion, certainly revealing but not decisive, says Oehler, but he understood nothing about the importance of the Karrer/Hollensteiner relationship. Scherrer kept on asking me *why* we, Karrer and I, went into Rustenschacher's store, to which I replied every time that I could not answer that question and that I simply could not understand how Scherrer could ask such a question, says Oehler. Scherrer kept on asking questions which, in my opinion, were unimportant questions, whereupon, of course, Scherrer received unimportant answers from me, says Oehler. These people keep on asking unimportant questions and for that reason keep on getting unimportant answers, but they are not aware of it. Just as they are not aware of the fact that the questions they ask are unimportant and as a result make no sense, it does not occur to them that the answers they receive to these questions are unimportant and make no sense. If I had not gone on mentioning Hollensteiner's name, says Oehler, Scherrer would not have hit upon Hollensteiner. There is something terribly depressing about sitting opposite a person who, by his very presence, continuously asserts that he is competent and yet has absolutely no competence in the matter at hand. We observe time and again, says Oehler, that we are with people who should be competent and who also assert and claim, indeed they go on claiming, to be competent in the matter for which we have come to them, whereas they are in an irresponsible, shattering, and really repugnant manner incompetent. Almost everybody we get together with about a matter, even if it is of the highest importance, is incompetent. Scherrer, says Oehler, is, in my opinion, the most incompetent when it's a question of Karrer, and the thought that Karrer is in Scherrer's hands, because Karrer is confined in Scherrer's section, is one of the most frightful thoughts. The enormous arrogance you sense, says Oehler, when you sit facing a man like Scherrer. Hardly a moment passes before you ask yourself what Karrer (the patient) really has to do with Scherrer (his doctor)? For a person like Karrer to be in the hands of a person like Scherrer is an unparalleled human monstrosity, says Oehler. But because we are familiar with his condition, it is immaterial to Karrer whether he is in Scherrer's hands or not. After all, the moment Karrer became finally mad it became immaterial whether Karrer was in Steinhof or not, says Oehler. But it is not the fact that a man like Scherrer is totally unphilosophical that is repugnant, says Oehler, although someone in Scherrer's position ought, first and foremost, besides having his medical knowledge, to be philosophical, it is his shameful ignorance. No matter what I say, Scherrer's ignorance repeatedly finds expression, says Oehler. Whenever I said something, no matter what it was, to Scherrer or whenever Scherrer responded to what I had said, no matter what it was, I was constantly aware that Scherrer's ignorance kept coming to light. But even when Scherrer says nothing, we hear nothing but ignorance from him, says Oehler, a person like Scherrer does not need to say something ignorant for us to know that we are dealing with a completely ignorant person. The observation that doctors are practicing in complete ignorance shakes us when we are with them, says Oehler. But among doctors, ignorance is a habit to which they have become accustomed over the centuries, says Oehler. Some exceptions notwithstanding, says Oehler. Scherrer's inability to think logically and thus to ask logical questions, give logical answers, and so forth, says Oehler, it was precisely when I was in his presence that it occurred to me that people like Scherrer can never go mad. As we know, psychiatric doctors do become mentally ill after a while, but not mad. Because they are ignorant of their life's theme these people finally become mentally ill, but never mad. As a result of incapacity, says Oehler, and basically because of their continual decades-long incompetence. And at that moment I again recognized to what degree madness is something that happens only among the highest orders of humanity. That at a given moment madness is *everything*. But to say something like that to Scherrer, says Oehler, would, above all else, be to overestimate Scherrer, so I quickly gave up the idea of saying anything to Scherrer such as what I have just said about the actual definition of madness, says Oehler. Scherrer is probably not the least bit interested in what took place in Rustenschacher's store, says Oehler, he only asked me to go up to Steinhof because he didn't know anything better to do, to ask me about what happened in Rustenschacher's store, says Oehler. Psychiatric doctors like to make a note of what you tell them, without worrying about it, and what you tell them is a matter of complete indifference to them, that is, it is a matter of complete indifference to them, and they do not worry about it. Because a psychiatric doctor has to make inquiries, they make inquiries, says Oehler, and of all the leads the ones they follow are the least important. Of course, the incident in Rustenschacher's store is not insignificant, says Oehler, but it is only one of hundreds of incidents that preceded the incident in Rustenschacher's store and that have the same importance as the one in Rustenschacher's store. Not a question about Hollensteiner, not a question about the people around Hollensteiner, not a question about Hollensteiner's place in modern science, not a question about Hollensteiner's philosophical circumstances, about his notes, never mind about Hollensteiner's relationship to Karrer or Karrer's to Hollensteiner. In the nature of things, Scherrer should have shown an interest in the time Hollensteiner and Karrer spent together at school, says Oehler, in their common route to school, their origins and so on, in their common, and their different, views and intentions and so on, says Oehler. The whole time I was there, Scherrer insisted that I only make statements about the incident in Rustenschacher's store, and on this point with regard to the happenings in Rustenschacher's store, says Oehler, Scherrer demanded the utmost precision from me. He kept saying leave nothing out, says Oehler, I can still hear him saying leave nothing out while I went on talking without a break about the incident in Rustenschacher's store. This incident acted as a so-called trigger incident, I said to Scherrer, says Oehler, but there can be no doubt that it is not a fundamental one. Scherrer did not react to my observation, I made the observation several times, says Oehler, and so I had repeatedly to take up the incident in Rustenschacher's store. That is absolutely grotesque,

Scherrer said on several occasions during my description of the incident in Rustenschacher's store. This statement was merely repugnant to me.

Oehler told Scherrer, among other things, that their, Oehler's and Karrer's, going into Rustenschacher's store was totally unpremeditated, we suddenly said, according to Oehler, let's go into Rustenschacher's store and immediately had them show us several of the thick, warm and at the same time sturdy winter trousers (according to Karrer). Rustenschacher's nephew, his salesman, Oehler told Scherrer, who had served us so often, pulled out a whole heap of trousers from the shelves that were all labeled with every possible official standard size and threw the trousers onto the counter, and Karrer had Rustenschacher's nephew hold all the trousers up to the light, while I stood to one side, the left-hand side near the mirror, as you look from the entrance door. And as was his, Karrer's, way, as Oehler told Scherrer, Karrer kept pointing with his walking stick and with greater and greater emphasis at the many thin spots that are revealed in these trousers if you hold them up to the light, Oehler told Scherrer, at the thin spots that really cannot be missed, as Karrer kept putting it, Oehler told Scherrer, Karrer simply kept saying these so-called new trousers, Oehler told Scherrer, while having the trousers held up to the light, and above all he kept on saying the whole time: these remarkably thin spots in these so-called new trousers, Oehler told Scherrer. He, Karrer, again let himself be carried away so far as to make the comment as to why these so-called new trousers—Karrer kept on saying so-called new trousers, over and over again, Oehler told Scherrer—why these so-called new trousers, which even if they were new, because they had not been worn, had nevertheless lain on one side for years and, on that account, no longer looked very attractive, something that he, Karrer, had no hesitation in telling Rustenschacher, just as he had no hesitation in telling Rustenschacher anything that had to do with the trousers that were lying on the counter and that Rustenschacher's nephew kept holding up to the light, it was not in his, Karrer's, nature to feel the least hesitation in saying the least thing about the trousers to Rustenschacher, just as he had no hesitation in saying a lot of things to Rustenschacher that did *not* concern the trousers, though it would surely be to his, Karrer's, advantage not to say many of the things to Rustenschacher that he had no hesitation in telling him, why the trousers should reveal these thin spots that no one could miss in a way that immediately aroused suspicion about the trousers. Karrer told Rustenschacher, Oehler told Scherrer, these very same new, though neglected, trousers which for that reason no longer looked very attractive, though they had never been worn, should reveal these thin spots, said Karrer to Rustenschacher, as Oehler told Scherrer. Perhaps it was that the material in question, of which the trousers were made, was an imported Czechoslovakian reject, Oehler told Scherrer. Karrer used the term Czechoslovakian reject several times, Oehler told Scherrer, and actually used it so often that Rustenschacher's nephew, the salesman, had to exercise the greatest self-control. Throughout the whole time we were in Rustenschacher's store, Rustenschacher himself busied himself labeling trousers, so Oehler told Scherrer. The salesman's self-control was always at a peak from the moment that we, Karrer and I, entered the store. Although from the moment we entered Rustenschacher's store everything pointed to a coming catastrophe (in Karrer), Oehler told Scherrer, I did not believe for one moment that it would really develop into such a, in the nature of things, hideous catastrophe for Karrer, as Oehler told Scherrer. However, I have observed the same thing on each of our visits to Rustenschacher's store, as Oehler told Scherrer: Rustenschacher's nephew exercised this sort of self-control for a long time, for the longest time, and in fact exercised this self-control up to the point when Karrer used the concept or the term Czechoslovakian reject. And Rustenschacher himself always exercised the utmost self-control during all our visits to his business, up to the moment, as Oehler told Scherrer, when Karrer suddenly, intentionally almost inaudibly but in this way all the more effectively, used the term or the concept Czechoslovakian reject. Every time, however, it was the salesman and Rustenschacher's nephew who first objected to the word reject, as Oehler told Scherrer. While the salesman, in the nature of things, in an angry tone of voice said to Karrer that the materials used in the trousers lying on the counter were neither rejects nor Czechoslovakian rejects but the very best of English materials, he threw the trousers he had just been holding up to the light onto the heap of other trousers, while Karrer was saying that it was all a matter of Czechoslovakian rejects, and made a move as if to go out of the store and into the office at the back of the store. It was always the same, Oehler told Scherrer: Karrer says, as quick as lightning, Czechoslovakian rejects, the salesman throws onto the heap the trousers that had just been held up and says angrily the very best English materials and makes a move as if to go out of the store and into the office at the back of the store, and in fact takes a few steps, as Oehler told Scherrer, toward Rustenschacher, but stops just in front of Rustenschacher, turns around and comes back to the counter, standing at which Karrer, holding his walking stick up in the air, says I have nothing against the way the trousers are finished, no I have nothing against the way the trousers are finished, I am not talking about the way the trousers are finished but about the quality of the materials, nothing against the workmanship, absolutely nothing against the workmanship. Understand me correctly, Karrer repeats several times to the salesman, as Oehler told Scherrer, I admit that the workmanship in these trousers is the very best, said Karrer, as Oehler told Scherrer, and Karrer immediately says to Rustenschacher's nephew, besides I have known Rustenschacher too long not to know that the workmanship is the best that anyone could imagine. But he, Karrer, could not refrain from remarking that we were dealing here with trouser materials, quite apart from the workmanship, with rejects and, as one could clearly see, with Czechoslovakian rejects, he simply had to repeat that in the case of these trouser materials we are dealing with Czechoslovakian rejects. Karrer suddenly raised his walking stick again, as Oehler told Scherrer, and banged several times loudly on the counter with his stick and said emphatically: you must admit that in the case of these trouser materials we are dealing with Czechoslovakian rejects! You must admit that! You must admit that! You must admit that! Whereupon Scherrer asks whether Karrer had said you must admit that several times and how loudly, to which I replied to Scherrer, five times, for still ringing in my ears was exactly how often Karrer had said you must admit that and I described to Scherrer exactly how loudly. Just at the moment when Karrer says you must admit that! and you must admit that gentlemen, and you must admit gentlemen that in the case of the trousers that are lying on the counter we are dealing with Czechoslovakian rejects, Rustenschacher's nephew again holds one of the pairs of trousers up to the light and it is, truth to tell, a pair with a particularly thin spot, I tell Scherrer, Oehler says, twice I repeat to Scherrer: with a particularly thin spot, with a particularly thin spot up to the light, I say, says Oehler, every one of these pairs of trousers that you show me here, says Karrer, Oehler tells Scherrer, is proof of the fact that in the case of all these trouser materials we are dealing with Czechoslovakian rejects. What was remarkable and astonishing and what made him suspicious at that moment, Oehler told Scherrer, was not the many thin spots in the trousers, nor the fact that in the case of these trousers we were dealing with rejects, and actually Czechoslovakian rejects, as he kept repeating, all of that was basically neither remarkable nor surprising and not astonishing either. What was remarkable, surprising, and astonishing was the fact, Karrer said to Rustenschacher's nephew, as Oehler told Scherrer, that a salesman, even if he were the nephew of the owner, would be upset by the truth that was told him, and he, Karrer, was telling nothing but the truth when he said that these trousers all had thin spots and that these materials were nothing but Czechoslovakian rejects, to which Rustenschacher's nephew replied, as Oehler told Scherrer, that he swore that in the case of the materials in question they were not dealing with Czechoslovakian rejects but with the most excellent English materials, several times the salesman swore to Karrer that in the case of the materials in question they were dealing with the most excellent English materials, most excellent, most excellent, not just excellent I keep on repeating, Oehler told Scherrer, again and again most excellent and not just excellent, because I was of the opinion that it is decisive whether you say excellent or most excellent, I keep telling Scherrer, actually in the case of the materials in question we are dealing with the most excellent English materials, says the salesman, Oehler told Scherrer, at which the salesman's, Rustenschacher's nephew's, voice, as I had to keep explaining to Scherrer, whenever he said the most excellent English materials, was uncomfortably high-pitched. If Rustenschacher's nephew's voice is of itself unpleasant, it is at its most unpleasant when he says the most excellent English materials, I know of no more unpleasant voice than Rustenschacher's nephew's voice when he says the most excellent English materials, Oehler told Scherrer. It is just that the materials are not labeled, says Rustenschacher's nephew, that makes it possible to sell them so cheaply, Oehler told Scherrer. These materials are deliberately not labeled as English materials, clearly to avoid paying duty, says Rustenschacher's nephew, and in the background Rustenschacher himself says, from the back of the store, as Oehler told Scherrer, these materials are not labeled so that they can come onto the market as cheaply as possible. Fifty percent of goods from England are not labeled, Rustenschacher told Karrer, I told Scherrer, says Oehler, and for this reason they are cheaper than the ones that are labeled, but as far as the quality goes there is absolutely no difference between goods that are labeled and ones that are not. The goods that are not labeled, especially in the case of textiles, are often forty, very often even fifty or sixty, percent cheaper than the ones that are labeled. As far as the purchaser, above all the consumer, is concerned it is a matter of complete indifference whether he is using labeled or unlabeled goods, it is a matter of complete indifference whether I am wearing a coat made of labeled, or whether I am wearing a coat made of unlabeled materials, says Rustenschacher from the back of the store, Oehler told Scherrer. As far as the customs are concerned we are, of course, dealing with rejects, as you say, Karrer, says Rustenschacher, so Oehler told Scherrer. It is very often the case that what are termed Czechoslovakian rejects, and declared as such to the customs authorities, are the most excellent English goods or most excellent goods from another foreign source, Rustenschacher said to Karrer. During this argument between Karrer and Rustenschacher, Rustenschacher's nephew kept holding up another pair of trousers to the light for Karrer, Oehler says to Scherrer. While I myself, so Oehler told Scherrer, totally uninvolved in the argument, was leaning on the counter, as I said totally uninvolved in the argument between Karrer and Rustenschacher. The two continued their argument, Oehler told Scherrer, just as if I were not in the store, and it was because of this that it was possible for me to observe the two of them with the greatest attention, in the process of which my main attention was, of course, focused on Karrer, for at this point I already feared him, Oehler told Scherrer. Once again I tell Scherrer, if you look from the entrance door, I was standing to the left of Karrer, once again I had to say, in front of the mirror, because Scherrer no longer knew that I had already told him once that during our whole stay in Rustenschacher's store I was always standing in front of the mirror. On the other hand, Scherrer did make a note of everything, according to Oehler, he even made a note of my repetitions, said Oehler. It was obviously a pleasure for Karrer to have all the trousers held up to the light, but having all the trousers held up to the light was nothing new for Karrer, and he refused to leave Rustenschacher's store until Rustenschacher's nephew had held all the trousers up to the light, Oehler told Scherrer, basically it was always the same scene when I went to Rustenschacher's store with Karrer but never so vehement, so incredibly intense, and, as we now know, culminating in such a terrible collapse on Karrer's part. Karrer took not the slightest notice of the impatience, the resentment, and the truly incessant anxiety on the part of Rustenschacher's nephew, Oehler told Scherrer. On the contrary, Karrer put Rustenschacher's nephew the salesman more and more to the test with ever new sadistic fabrications conspicuously aimed at him. Rustenschacher's nephew always reacted too slowly for Karrer. You react too slowly for me said Karrer several times, says Oehler to Scherrer, basically you have no ability to react, it is a mystery to me how you find yourself in a position to serve me, how you find yourself in a position to work in this truly excellent store of your uncle's, Karrer said several times to Rustenschacher's nephew, Oehler told Scherrer. While you are holding two pairs of trousers up to the light, I can hold up ten pairs, Karrer said to Rustenschacher's nephew. How unhappy Rustenschacher was about the argument between Karrer and his, Rustenschacher's, nephew is shown by the fact that Rustenschacher left the store on several occasions and went into the office, apparently to avoid having to take part in the painful argument. I myself was afraid that I would have to intervene in the argument at any moment, then Karrer raised his walking stick again, banged it on the counter, and said, to all appearances we are dealing with a state of exhaustion, it is possible that we are dealing with a state of exhaustion, but I cannot be bothered at all with such a state of exhaustion, cannot be bothered at all, he said to himself, while he was banging on the counter with his walking stick, in the particular rhythm with which he always banged on the counter in Rustenschacher's store, apparently to calm his inner state of excitement, Oehler told Scherrer, and then he, Karrer, began once more to heap his excesses of assertion and insinuation concerning the trousers on the head of the salesman. Rustenschacher certainly heard everything from the back of the store, as Oehler told Scherrer, even if it appeared as though Rustenschacher observed nothing happening between Karrer and his nephew, Rustenschacher's self-control, I told Scherrer, said Oehler, was at an absolute peak, as the argument between Karrer and Rustenschacher's nephew heated up, Rustenschacher had to exercise a degree of self-control that would have been impossible in another human being. *But the way* in which Karrer had behaved at certain times in Rustenschacher's store and because Rustenschacher *knew* how Karrer always *acts in this almost unbearable manner* in Rustenschacher's store and Rustenschacher knew how Karrer always *re*acts to everything, but he knew that he had nevertheless always calmed down in the end, in fact, whenever we had gone into Rustenschacher's store, Rustenschacher had always shown a much greater ability to judge Karrer's state of mind than Scherrer. Suddenly Karrer said to Rustenschacher, Oehler told Scherrer, if you, Rustenschacher, take up a position behind the pair of trousers that your nephew is at this moment holding up to the light for me, immediately behind this pair of trousers that your nephew is holding up to the light for me, I can see your face through this pair of trousers with a clarity with which I do not wish to see your face. But Rustenschacher controlled himself. Whereupon Karrer said, enough trousers! enough materials! enough! Oehler told Scherrer. Immediately after this, however, Oehler told Scherrer, Karrer repeated that with regard to the materials that were lying on the counter they were dealing one hundred percent with Czechoslovakian rejects. Aside from the workmanship, says Karrer, Oehler told Scherrer, as far as these materials were concerned, it was quite obviously a question, even to the layman, of Czechoslovakian rejects. The workmanship is the best, of course, the workmanship is the best, Karrer keeps repeating, that has always been apparent in all the years that I have been coming to Rustenschacher's store. And how long had he been coming to Rustenschacher's store? and how many pairs of trousers had he already bought in Rustenschacher's store? says Karrer, Oehler tells Scherrer, not one button has come off, says Karrer, Oehler told Scherrer. Not a single seam has come undone! says Karrer to Rustenschacher. My sister, says Karrer, has never yet had to sew on a button that has come off, says Karrer, it is true that my sister has never yet had to sew on a single button that has come off a pair of trousers I bought from you, Rustenschacher, because all the buttons that have been sewn onto the trousers I bought from you are really sewn on so securely that no one can tear one of these buttons off. And not a single seam has come undone in all these years in any of the pairs of trousers I have bought in your store! Scherrer noted what I was saying in the so-called shorthand that is customary among psychiatric doctors. And I felt terrible to be sitting here in Pavilion VI in front of Scherrer and making these statements about Karrer, while Karrer is confined in Pavilion VII, we say *confined* because we don't want to say *locked up* or *locked up like an animal*, says Oehler. Here I am sitting in Pavilion VI and talking about Karrer in Pavilion VII without Karrer's knowing anything about the fact that I am sitting in Pavilion VI and talking about him in Pavilion VII. And, of course, I did not visit Karrer, when I went *into* Steinhof, nor when I came *away from* Steinhof, says Oehler. But Karrer probably couldn't have been visited. Visiting patients confined in Pavilion VII is not permitted, says Oehler. No one in Pavilion VII is allowed to have visitors. Suddenly Rustenschacher says,

I tell Scherrer, says Oehler, that Karrer can try to tear a button off the trousers that are lying on the counter. Or try to rip open one of these seams! says Rustenschacher to Karrer, subject all of these pairs of trousers to a thorough examination, says Rustenschacher, and Rustenschacher invites Karrer to tear, to pull, and to tug at all the pairs of trousers lying on the counter in any way he likes, Oehler told Scherrer. Rustenschacher invited Karrer to do whatever he liked to the trousers. Possibly, Rustenschacher was thinking pedagogically at that moment, Oehler said to Scherrer. Then Oehler said to Rustenschacher that he, Karrer, would refrain when so directly invited to tear up all these pairs of Rustenschacher's trousers, Oehler told Scherrer. I prefer not to make such a tear test, said Karrer to Rustenschacher, Oehler told Scherrer. For if I did make the attempt, said Karrer, to rip *open* a seam or even tear a button *off* just one pair of these trousers, people would at once say that I was mad, and I am on my guard against this, because you should be on your guard against being called mad, Oehler told Scherrer. But if I really were to tear these trousers, Karrer said to Rustenschacher and his nephew, I would tear all of these trousers into rags in the shortest possible time, to say nothing of the fact that I would tear all the buttons off all of these trousers. Such rashness to invite me to tear up all these trousers! says Karrer. Such rashness!, Oehler told Scherrer. Then Karrer returned to the thin spots, Oehler told Scherrer, saying that it was remarkable that if you held all of these trousers up to the light, thin spots were to be seen, thin spots that were quite typical of reject materials, says Karrer. Whereupon Rustenschacher's nephew says, one should not, as anyone knows, hold up a pair of trousers to the light, because all trousers if held up to the light show thin spots. Show me one pair of trousers in the world that you can hold up to the light, says Rustenschacher to Karrer from the back. Not even the newest, not even the newest, says Rustenschacher, Oehler told Scherrer. In every case you would find at least one thin spot in a pair of trousers held up to the light, says Rustenschacher's nephew, says Oehler to Scherrer. Suddenly Rustenschacher adds from the back: every piece of *woven goods* reveals a thin spot when held up to the light, a thin spot. To which Karrer replies that every intelligent shopper naturally holds an article that he has chosen to buy up to the light if he doesn't want to be swindled, Oehler told Scherrer. Every article, no matter what, must be held up to the light if you want to buy it, Karrer said. Even if merchants fear nothing so much as having their articles held up to the light, said Karrer, Oehler told Scherrer. But naturally there are trouser materials and thus trousers, I tell Scherrer, that you can hold up to the light without further ado if you are really dealing with excellent materials, I say, you can hold them up to the light without further ado. But apparently, I tell Scherrer, according to Oehler, we were dealing with English materials in the case of the materials in question and not, as Karrer thought, with Czechoslovakian, and hence not with Czechoslovakian rejects, but I do not believe that we were dealing with excellent, or indeed most excellent English materials, I tell Scherrer, for I saw the thin spots myself in all of these trousers, except that naturally I would not have held forth in the way that Karrer held forth about those thin spots in all the trousers, I tell Scherrer. Probably I would not have gone into Rustenschacher's store at all, seeing that we had been in Rustenschacher's store two or three days before the visit to Rustenschacher's store. It was the same the time before last when we went in: Karrer had Rustenschacher's nephew hold the trousers up to the light, but not so many pairs of trousers, after just a short time Karrer says, thank you, I'm not going to buy any trousers, and to me, let's go, and we leave Rustenschacher's store. But now the situation was totally different. Karrer was already in a state of excitement when he entered Rustenschacher's store because we had been talking about Hollensteiner the whole way from Klosterneuburgerstrasse to Albersbachstrasse, Karrer had become more and more excited as we made our way, and at the peak of his excitement, I had never seen Karrer so excited before, we went into Rustenschacher's store. Of course we should not have gone into Rustenschacher's store in such a high state of excitement, I tell Scherrer. It would have been better not to go into Rustenschacher's store but to go back to Klosterneuburgerstrasse, but Karrer did not take up my suggestion of returning to Klosterneuburgerstrasse. I have made up my mind to go into Rustenschacher's store, Karrer says to me, Oehler told Scherrer, and as Karrer's tone of voice had the character of an irreversible command, I tell Scherrer, says Oehler, I had no choice but to go into Rustenschacher's store with Karrer on this occasion. And I could never have let Karrer go into Rustenschacher's store on his own, says Oehler, not in that state. It was clear to me that we were taking a risk in going into Rustenschacher's store, I tell Scherrer, Karrer's state prevented me from saying a word against his intention of going into Rustenschacher's store. If you know Karrer's nature, I tell Scherrer, says Oehler, you know that if Karrer says he is going into Rustenschacher's store it is pointless trying to do anything about it. No matter what Karrer's intention was, when he was in such a condition there was no way of stopping him, no way of persuading him to do otherwise. On the one hand, it was Rustenschacher who let him go into Rustenschacher's store, on the other hand Rustenschacher's nephew, both of them were basically repugnant to him, just as, basically, everyone was repugnant to him, even I was repugnant to him: you have to know that everyone was repugnant to him, even those with whom he consorted of his own volition, if you consorted with him of his own volition, you were not exempted from the fact that everybody was repugnant to Karrer, I tell Scherrer, says Oehler. *There is no one with such great sensitivity. No one with such fluctuations of consciousness. No one so easily irritated and so ready to be hurt,* I tell Scherrer, says Oehler. The truth is Karrer felt he was constantly being watched, and he always reacted as if he felt he was constantly being watched, and for this reason he never had a single moment's peace. This constant restlessness is also what distinguishes him from everyone else, if constant restlessness can distinguish a person, I tell Scherrer, Oehler says. And to be with a constantly restless person who imagines that he is restless even when he is in reality not restless is the most difficult thing, I tell Scherrer, says Oehler. Even when nothing suggested one or more causes of restlessness, when nothing suggested the least restlessness, Karrer was restless because he had the feeling (the sense) that he was restless, because he had reason to, as he thought. The theory according to which a person is everything he imagines himself to be could be studied in Karrer, the way he always imagined, and he probably imagined this all his life, that he was critically ill without knowing what the illness was that made him critically ill, and probably because of this, and certainly according to the theory, I tell Scherrer, says Oehler, he really was critically ill. *When we imagine ourselves to be in a state of mind,* no matter what, we are in that state of mind, and thus in that state of illness which we imagine ourselves to be in, *in every state that we imagine ourselves in*. And we do not allow ourselves to be disturbed in what we imagine, I tell Scherrer, and thus we do not allow what we have imagined to be negated by anything, especially by *anything external*. What incredible self-confidence, on the one hand, and what incredible weakness of character and helplessness, on the other, psychiatric doctors show, I think, while I am sitting opposite Scherrer and making these statements about Karrer and, in particular, about Karrer's behavior in Rustenschacher's store, says Oehler. After a short time I ask myself why I am sitting opposite Scherrer and making these statements and giving this information about Karrer. But I do not spend long thinking about this question, so as not to give Scherrer an opportunity of starting to have thoughts about my unusual behavior towards him, because I had declared myself ready to tell him as much as possible about Karrer that afternoon. I now think it would have been better to get up and leave, without bothering about what Scherrer is thinking, if I were to leave in spite of my assurance that I would talk about Karrer for an hour or two I thought, Oehler says. If only I could go outside, I said to myself while I was sitting opposite Scherrer, out of this terrible whitewashed and barred room, and go away. Go away as far as possible. But, like everyone who sits facing a psychiatric doctor, I had only the one thought, that of not arousing any sort of suspicion in the person sitting opposite me about my own mental condition and that means about my soundness of mind. I thought that basically I was acting against Karrer by going to Scherrer, says Oehler. My conscience was suddenly *not clear*, do you know what it means to have a sudden feeling that your conscience is not clear with respect to a friend? and it makes things all the worse if your friend is in Karrer's position, I thought. To speak merely of a bad conscience would be to water the feeling down quite inadmissibly, says Oehler, I was ashamed. For there was no doubt in my mind that Scherrer was an enemy of Karrer's, but I only became aware of this *after a long time, after long observation* of Scherrer—whom I have *known* for years, ever since Karrer was first in Steinhof—and it was only because we were acquainted that I agreed to pay a call on him, but he was not so well known to me that I could say this is someone I know, in that case I would not have accepted Scherrer's invitation to go to Steinhof and make a statement about Karrer. I thought several times about getting up and leaving, says Oehler, but then I stopped thinking that way, I said to myself it *doesn't matter*. Scherrer makes me uneasy because he is so superficial. If I had originally imagined that I was going to visit a scientific man, in the shape of a scientific doctor, I soon recognized that I was sitting across from a charlatan. Too often we recognize too late that we should not have become involved in something that unexpectedly debases us. On the other hand, I had to assume that Scherrer is performing a useful function for Karrer, says Oehler, but I saw more and more that Scherrer, although he is described as the opposite and although he himself believes in this opposite, is indeed convinced by it, is an enemy of Karrer's, a doctor in a white coat playing the role of a benefactor. To Scherrer, Karrer is nothing more than an object that he misuses. Nothing more than a victim. Nauseated by Scherrer, I tell him that Karrer says that there really are trousers and trouser materials that can be held up to the light, *but these*, says Karrer and bursts out into a laughter that is quite uncharacteristic of Karrer, because it is characteristic of Karrer's madness, *you don't need to hold these trousers up to the light*, Karrer says, banging on the counter with his walking stick at the same time, *to see that we are dealing with Czechoslovakian rejects*. Now for the first time I noticed quite clear signs of madness, I tell Scherrer, whereupon, as I can see, Scherrer immediately makes a note, says Oehler, because I am watching all that Scherrer is noting down, says Oehler, *Oehler* (in other words, I) is saying at this moment: *for the first time quite clear signs of madness*; I observe *not only how Scherrer reacts, I also observe what Scherrer makes notes of and how Scherrer makes notes*. I am not surprised, says Oehler, that Scherrer underlines my comment *for the first time signs of madness*. It is merely proof of his incompetence, says Oehler. It occurred to me that Rustenschacher was still labeling trousers in the back, I told Scherrer, and I thought it's incomprehensible, and thus uncanny, that Rustenschacher should be labeling so many pairs of trousers. Possibly it was a sudden, unbelievable increase in Karrer's state of excitement that prompted Rustenschacher's incessant labeling of trousers, for Rustenschacher's incessant labeling of trousers was gradually irritating even me. I thought that Rustenschacher really never sells as many pairs of trousers as he labels, I suddenly tell Scherrer, but he probably also supplies other smaller businesses in the outlying districts, in the twenty-first, twenty-second, and twenty-third districts, in which you can also buy Rustenschacher's trousers and thus Rustenschacher also plays the role of a trousers wholesaler for a number of such textile firms in outlying districts. Now, Karrer says, in the case of this pair of trousers that you are now holding right in front of my face instead of holding them up to the light, Oehler tells Scherrer, it is clearly a case of Czechoslovakian rejects. It was simply because Karrer did not insult Rustenschacher's nephew to his face with this new objection to Rustenschacher's trousers, Oehler told Scherrer. Karrer had at first prolonged his visit to

Rustenschacher's store because of the pains in his leg, I told Scherrer, says Oehler. Apparently we had walked too far before we entered Rustenschacher's store, and not only too far but also too quickly while at the same time carrying on a most exhausting conversation about Wittgenstein, I tell Scherrer, says Oehler, I mention the name on purpose, because I knew that Scherrer had never heard the name before, and this was confirmed at once, in the very moment that I said the name Wittgenstein, says Oehler, however, at that point Karrer had probably not been thinking about his painful legs for a long time, but simply for the reason that I could not leave him I was unable to leave Rustenschacher's store. This is something we often observe in ourselves when we are in a room (any room you care to mention): we seem chained to the room (any room you care to mention) and have to stay there, because we cannot leave it when we are *upset*. Karrer probably wanted to leave Rustenschacher's store, I tell Scherrer, says Oehler, but Karrer no longer had the strength to do so. And I myself was no longer capable of taking Karrer out of Rustenschacher's store at the crucial moment. After Rustenschacher had repeated, as his nephew had before him, that the trouser materials with which we were dealing were excellent, he did not, like his nephew before him, say most excellent, just excellent, materials and that it was senseless to maintain that we were dealing with rejects or even with Czechoslovakian rejects, Karrer once again says that in the case of these trousers they were apparently dealing with Czechoslovakian rejects, and he made as if to take a deep breath, as it seemed unsuccessfully, whereupon he wanted to say something else, I tell Scherrer, says Oehler, but he, Karrer, was out of breath and was unable, because he was out of breath, to say what he apparently wanted to say.

These thin spots. These thin spots. These thin spots. These thin spots. These thin spots over and over again. *These thin spots. These thin spots. These thin spots*, incessantly. *These thin spots. These thin spots. These thin spots.* Rustenschacher had immediately grasped what was happening and, on my orders, Rustenschacher's nephew had already ordered everything to be done that had to be done, Oehler tells Scherrer.

The unbelievable sensitivity of a person like Karrer on the one hand and his great ruthlessness on the other, said Oehler. On the one hand, his overwhelming wealth of feeling and on the other his overwhelming brutality. There is a constant tussle between all the possibilities of human thought and between all the possibilities of a human mind's sensitivity and between all the possibilities of a human character, says Oehler. On the other hand we are in a state of constant *completely natural* and not for a moment *artificial* intellectual preparedness when we are with a person like Karrer. We acquire an increasingly radical and, in fact, an increasingly more radically clear view of and relationship to all objects even if these objects are the sort of objects that in normal circumstances human beings cannot grasp. What until now, until the moment we meet a person like Karrer, we found unattainable we suddenly find attainable and transparent. Suddenly the world no longer consists of layers of darkness but is totally layered in clarity, says Oehler. It is in the recognition of this and in the constant readiness to recognize this, says Oehler, that the difficulties of constantly being with a person like Karrer lie. A person like that is, of course, feared because he is afraid (of being transparent). We are now concerned with a person like Karrer because now he has actually been taken away from us (by being taken into Steinhof). If Karrer were not at this moment in Steinhof and if we did not know for certain that he is in Steinhof, were this not an absolute certainty for us, we would not dare to talk about Karrer, but because Karrer has gone finally mad, as we know, which we know not because science has confirmed it but simply because we only need to use our heads, and what we have ascertained by using our own heads and what, furthermore, science has confirmed for us, for there is no doubt that in Scherrer, says Oehler, we are dealing with a typical representative of science, which Karrer always called *so-called* science, we do dare to talk about Karrer. Just as Karrer, in general, says Oehler, called everything so-called, there was nothing that he did not call only so-called, nothing that he would not have called so-called, and by so doing his powers achieved an unbelievable force. He, Karrer, had never said, says Oehler, even if on the contrary he did say it frequently and in many cases incessantly, in such incessantly spoken words and in such incessantly used concepts, that it was not a question of science, always only of so-called science, it was not a question of art, only of so-called art, not of technology, only of so-called technology, not of illness, only of so-called illness, not of knowledge, only of so-called knowledge, while saying that everything was only so-called he reached an unbelievable potential and an unparalleled credibility. When we are dealing with people we are only dealing with so-called people, just as when we are dealing with facts we are only dealing with so-called facts, just as the whole of matter, since it only emanates from the human mind, is only so-called matter, just as we know that everything emanates from the human mind and from nothing else, if we understand *the concept knowledge* and accept it as a concept that we understand. This is what we go on thinking of and we constantly *substantiate* everything on this basis and on no other. That on this basis things, and things in themselves, are only so-called or, to be completely accurate, only so-called so-called, to use Karrer's words, says Oehler, goes without saying. The structure of the whole is, as we know, a *completely simple one* and if we always accept this completely simple structure as our starting point we shall make progress. If we do not accept this completely simple structure of the whole as our starting point, we have what we call a complete standstill, but also *a whole as a so-called whole*. How could I dare, said Karrer, not to call something only so-called and so draw up an account and design a world, no matter how big and no matter how sensible or how foolish, if I were always only to say to myself (and to act accordingly) that we are dealing with what is so-called and then, over and over again, a so-called so-called something. Just as behavior in its repetition as in its absoluteness is only so-called behavior, Karrer said, says Oehler. Just as we have only a so-called position to adopt vis-à-vis everything we understand and vis-à-vis everything we do not understand, but which we think is real and thus true. Walking with Karrer was an unbroken series of thought processes, says Oehler, which we often developed in juxtaposition one to the other and would then suddenly unjoin them somewhere along the way, when we had reached a place for *standing* or a place for *thinking*, but generally at one particular place for *standing and thinking* when it was a question, says Oehler, of making one of my thoughts into a single one, with another one (his) not into a double one, for a double thought is, as we know, impossible and therefore nonsense. There is never anything but one single thought, just as it is wrong to say that there is a thought beside this thought and what, in such a constellation, is often called a secondary thought, which is sheer nonsense. If Karrer had a thought, and I myself had a thought, and it must be said that we were constantly finding ourselves in that state because it had long since ceased to be possible for us to be in any state but that state, we both constantly had a thought, or, as Karrer would have said, even if he didn't say it, a so-called constant thought right up to the moment when we dared to make our two separate thoughts into a single one, just as we maintain that about really great thoughts, that is so-called really great thoughts, which are, however, not thoughts, for a so-called really great thought is never *a* thought, it is a summation of all thoughts pertaining to a so-called great matter, thus there is no such thing as the really great thought, we do not dare, we told ourselves in such a case, says Oehler, when we had been walking together for a long time and had had *one* thought each individually, but side by side, and when we had held on to this thought and seen through it to make these two completely transparent thoughts into one. That was, one could say, nothing but playfulness, but then you could say that everything is only playfulness, says Oehler, that no matter what we are dealing with we are dealing with playfulness is also a possibility, says Oehler, but I do not contemplate that. The thought is quite right, says Oehler, when we are standing in front of the Obenaus Inn, *suddenly* stopping in front of the Obenaus, is what Oehler says: the thought that Karrer will never go out to Obenaus again is quite right. Karrer really will not go out to Obenaus again, because he will not come out of Steinhof again. We know that Karrer will not come out of Steinhof again, and thus we know that he will not go into Obenaus again. *What will he miss by not going?* we immediately ask ourselves, says Oehler, if we get involved with this question, although we know that it is senseless to have asked this question, but if the question has once been asked, let us consider it and approach the response to the question, *What will Karrer miss by not going into Obenaus again?* It is easy enough to ask the question, but the answer is, however, complicated, for we cannot answer a question like, *What will Karrer miss if he does not go into Obenaus again?* with a simple *yes* or a simple *no.* Although we know that it would have been simpler not to have asked ourselves the question (it doesn't matter what question), we have nevertheless asked ourselves the (and thus a) question. We have asked ourselves an incredibly complicated question and done so completely consciously, says Oehler, because we *think* it is possible for us to answer even a complicated question, we are not afraid to answer such a complicated question as *What will Karrer miss if he does not go into Obenaus again?* Because we think we know so much (and in such depth) about Karrer that we can answer the question, *What will Karrer miss if he does not go into Obenaus again?* Thus we do not dare to answer the question, *we know* that we can answer it, we are not risking anything with this question although it is only as we come to the realization that we are risking nothing with this question that we realize that we are risking *everything* and not only with this question. I would not, however, go so far as to say that I can *explain* how I answer the question, *What will Karrer miss if he does not go into Obenaus again?* says Oehler, but I will also not answer the question without explanation and indeed not without explanation of how I have answered the question or of how I came to ask the question at all. If we want to answer a question like the question, *What will Karrer miss if he does not go into Obenaus again?* we have to answer it *ourselves,* but this presupposes a complete knowledge of Karrer's circumstances with relation to Obenaus and thereafter, of course, the full knowledge of everything connected with Karrer and with Obenaus, by which means we arrive at the fact that we cannot answer the question, *What will Karrer miss if he does not go into Obenaus again?* The assertion that we answer the question while answering it is thus a false one, because we have probably answered the question and, as we believe and know, have answered it ourselves, we haven't answered it at all, because we have simply not answered the question ourselves, because it is not possible to answer a question like the question, *What will Karrer miss if he does not go into Obenaus again?* Because we have not asked the question, *Will Karrer go into Obenaus again?* which could be answered simply by yes or no, in the actual case in point by answering no, and would thus cause ourselves no difficulty, but instead we are asking, *What will Karrer miss if he does not go into Obenaus again?* it is automatically a question that cannot be answered, says Oehler. Apart from that, we do, however, answer this question when we call the question that we asked ourselves a so-called question and the answer that we give a so-called answer. While we are again *acting* within the framework of the concept of the so-called and are thus *thinking*, it seems to us quite possible to answer the question, *What will Karrer miss if he does not go into Obenaus again?* But the question, *What will Karrer miss if he does not go into Obenaus again?* can also be applied to *me*. I can ask, *What will I miss if I do not go into Obenaus again?* or you can ask yourself, *What will I miss if I do not go into Obenaus again?* but at the same time it is most highly probable that one of these days I will indeed go into Obenaus again and you will probably go into Obenaus again to eat or drink something, says Oehler. I can say *in my opinion* Karrer will not go into Obenaus again, I can even say Karrer will *probably* not go into Obenaus again, I can say *with certainty* or *definitely* that Karrer will not go into Obenaus again. But I cannot ask, *What will Karrer miss by the fact that he will not go into Obenaus again?* because I cannot answer the question. But let's simply make the *attempt* to ask ourselves, *What does a person who has often been to Obenaus miss if he suddenly does not go into Obenaus any more (and indeed never again)?* says Oehler. Suppose such a person simply never goes among the people who are sitting there, says Oehler. When we ask it in this way, we see that we cannot answer the question because in the meantime we have expanded it by an endless number of other questions. If, nevertheless, we do ask, says Oehler, and we start with the people who are sitting in Obenaus. We first ask, *What is or who is sitting in Obenaus?* so that we can then ask, *Whom does someone who suddenly does not go into Obenaus again (ever again) miss?* Then we at once ask ourselves, *With which of the people sitting in Obenaus shall I begin?* and so on. Look, says Oehler, we can ask any question we like, we cannot answer the question if we *really* want to answer it, to this extent there is not a single question in the whole conceptual world that can be answered. But in spite of this, millions and millions of questions are constantly being asked and answered by questions, as we know, and those who ask the questions and those who answer are not bothered by whether it is wrong because they cannot be bothered, so as not to stop, so that there shall suddenly be nothing more, says Oehler. Here, in front of Obenaus, look, here, up there on the fourth floor, I once lived in a room, a very small room, when I came back from America, says Oehler. He'd come back from America and had said to himself, you should take a room in the place where you lived thirty years ago in the ninth district, and he had taken a room in the ninth district in the Obenaus. But suddenly he couldn't stand it any longer, not in this street any longer, not in this city any longer, says Oehler. During his stay in America, everything had changed in the city in which *he was suddenly living again after thirty years* in what for him was a horrible way. I hadn't reckoned on that, says Oehler. I suddenly realized that there was nothing left for me in this city, says Oehler, but now that I had, as it happened, returned to it and, to tell the truth, with the intention of staying *forever*, I was not able immediately to turn around and go back to America. For I had really left America with the intention of leaving America forever, says Oehler. I realized, on the one hand, that there was nothing left for me in Vienna, says Oehler and, on the other, I realized with all the acuity of my intellect that there was also nothing more left for me in America, and he had walked through the city for days and weeks and months pondering how he would commit suicide. For it was clear to me that I must commit suicide, says Oehler, completely and utterly clear, only not *how* and also not exactly *when*, but it was clear to me that it would be *soon*, because it had to be soon. He went into the inner city again and again, says Oehler, and stood in front of the front doors of the inner city and looked for a particular name from his childhood and his youth, a name that was either loved or feared, but which was known to him, but he did not find a single one of these names. Where have all these people gone who are associated with the names that are familiar to me, but which I cannot find on any of these doors? I asked myself, says Oehler. He kept on asking himself this question for weeks and for months. We often go on asking the same question for months at a time, he says, ask ourselves or ask others but above all we ask ourselves and when, even after the longest time, even after the passage of years, we have still not been able to answer this question because it is not possible for us to answer it, it doesn't matter what the question is, says Oehler, we ask another, a new, question, but perhaps again a question that we have already asked ourselves, and so it goes on throughout life, until the mind can stand it no longer. Where have all these people, friends, relatives, enemies gone to? he had asked himself and had gone on and on looking for names, even at night this questioning about the names had given him no peace. Were there not hundreds and thousands of names? he had asked himself. Where are all these people with whom I had contact thirty years ago? he asked himself. If only I were to meet just a single one of these people. Where have they gone to? he asked himself incessantly, and why. Suddenly it became clear to him that all the people he was looking for no longer existed. These people no longer exist, he suddenly thought, there's no sense in looking for these people because they no longer exist, he suddenly said to himself, and he gave up his room in Obenaus and went into the mountains, into the country. I went into the mountains, says Oehler, but I couldn't stand it in the mountains either and came back into the city again. I have often stood here with Karrer beneath the Obenaus, says Oehler, and talked to him about all these frightful associations. Then we, Oehler and I, were on the Friedensbrücke. Oehler tells me that Karrer's proposal to explain one of Wittgenstein's statements to him on the Friedensbrücke came to nothing; because he was so exhausted, Karrer did not even mention Wittgenstein's name again on the Friedensbrücke. I myself was not capable of mentioning Ferdinand Ebner's name any more, says Oehler. In recent times we have very often found ourselves in a state of exhaustion in which we were no longer able to explain what we intended to explain. We used the Friedensbrücke to relieve our states of exhaustion, says Oehler. There were two statements we wanted to explain to each other, says Oehler, I wanted to explain to Karrer a statement of Wittgenstein's that was completely unclear to him, and Karrer wanted to explain a statement by Ferdinand Ebner that was completely unclear to me. But because we were exhausted we were suddenly no longer capable, there on the Friedensbrücke, of saying the names of Wittgenstein and Ferdinand Ebner because we had brought our walking and our thinking, the one out of the other, to an incredible, almost unbearable, state of nervous tension. We had already thought that this practice of bringing walking and thinking to the point of the most terrible nervous tension could not go on for long without causing harm, and in fact we were unable to carry on the practice, says Oehler. Karrer had to put up with the consequences, I myself was so weakened by Karrer's, I have to say, complete nervous breakdown, for that is how I can unequivocally describe Karrer's madness, as a fatal structure of the brain, that I can no longer say the word Wittgenstein on the Friedensbrücke, let alone say anything about Wittgenstein or anything connected with Wittgenstein, says Oehler, looking at the traffic on the Friedensbrücke. Whereas we always thought we could make walking and thinking *into a single total process*, even for a fairly long time, I now have to say that it is impossible to make walking and thinking into one total process for a fairly long period of time. For, in fact, it is not possible *to walk and to think with the same intensity for a fairly long period of time*, sometimes we walk more intensively, but think less intensively, then we think intensively and do not walk as intensively as we are thinking, sometimes we think with a much higher presence of mind than we walk with and sometimes we walk with a far higher presence of mind than we think with, but we cannot walk and think with the same presence of mind, says Oehler, just as we cannot walk and think with the same intensity over a fairly long period of time and make walking and thinking for a fairly long period of time into a total whole with a total equality of value. If we walk more intensively, our thinking lets up, says Oehler, if we think more intensively, our walking does. On the other hand, we have to walk in order to be able to think, says Oehler, just as we have to think in order to be able to walk, the one derives from the other and the one derives from the other with ever-increasing skill. But never beyond the point of exhaustion. We cannot say we think the way we walk, just as we cannot say we walk the way we think because we cannot walk the way we think, cannot think the way we walk. If we are walking intensively for a long time deep in an intensive thought, says Oehler, then we soon have to stop walking or stop thinking, because it is not possible to walk and to think with the same intensity for a fairly long period of time. Of course, we can say that we succeed in walking evenly and in thinking evenly, but this art is apparently the most difficult and one that we are least able to master. We say of one person he is an excellent thinker and we say of another person he is an excellent walker, but we cannot say of any one person that he is an excellent (or first-rate) thinker and walker at the same time. On the other hand walking and thinking are two completely similar concepts, and we can readily say (and maintain) that the person who walks and thus the person who, for example, walks excellently also thinks excellently, just as the person who thinks, and thus thinks excellently, also walks excellently. If we observe very carefully someone who is walking, we also know how he thinks. If we observe very carefully someone who is thinking, we know how he walks. If we observe most minutely someone walking over a fairly long period of time, we gradually come to know his way of thinking, the structure of his thought, just as we, if we observe someone over a fairly long period of time as to the way he thinks, we will gradually come to know how he walks. So observe, over a fairly long period of time, someone who is thinking and then observe how he walks, or, vice versa, observe someone walking over a fairly long period of time and then observe how he thinks. There is nothing more revealing than to see a thinking person walking, just as there is nothing more revealing than to see a walking person thinking, in the process of which we can easily say that we see how the walker thinks just as we can say that we see how the thinker walks, because we are seeing the thinker walking and conversely seeing the walker thinking, and so on, says Oehler. Walking and thinking are in a perpetual relationship that is based on trust, says Oehler. The science of walking and the science of thinking are basically a single science. How does this person walk and how does he think! we often ask ourselves as though coming to a conclusion, without actually asking ourselves this question as though coming to a conclusion, just as we often ask the question in order to come to a conclusion (without actually asking it), how does this person think, how does this person walk! Whenever I see someone thinking, can I therefore infer from this how he walks? I ask myself, says Oehler, if I see someone walking can I infer how he thinks? No, of course, I *may* not ask myself this question, for this question is one of those questions that *may* not be asked because they *cannot* be asked without being nonsense. But naturally we may not reproach someone who walks, whose walking we have analyzed, for his thinking, before we know his thinking. Just as we may not reproach someone who thinks for his walking before we know his walking. *How carelessly this person walks* we often think and very often *how carelessly this person thinks,* and we soon come to realize that this person walks in exactly the same way as he thinks, thinks the same way as he walks. However, we may not ask *ourselves* how we walk, for then we walk differently from the way we really walk and our walking simply cannot be judged, just as we may not ask ourselves how we think, for then we cannot judge how we think because it is no longer *our* thinking. Whereas, of course, we can observe someone else without his knowledge (or his being aware of it) and observe how he walks or thinks, that is, his walking and his thinking, we can never observe ourselves without our knowledge (or our being aware of it). If we observe ourselves, we are never observing ourselves but someone else. Thus we can never talk about self-observation, or when we talk about the fact that we observe ourselves we are talking as someone we never are when we are not observing ourselves, and thus when we observe ourselves we are never observing the person we intended to observe but someone else. The concept of self-observation and so, also, of self-description is thus false. Looked at in this light, all concepts (ideas), says Oehler, like self-observation, self-pity, self-accusation and so on, are false. We ourselves do not see ourselves, it is never possible for us to see ourselves. But we also cannot explain to someone else (a different object) what he *is* like, because we can only tell him *how we see him,* which probably coincides with what he is but which we cannot explain in such a way as to say *this is how he is.* Thus everything is something quite different from what it is for us, says Oehler. And always something quite different from what it is for everything else. Quite apart from the fact that even the designations with which we designate things are quite different from the actual ones. To that extent all designations are wrong, says Oehler. But when we entertain such thoughts, he says, we soon see that we are lost in these thoughts. We are lost in every thought if we surrender ourselves to that thought, even if we surrender ourselves to one single thought, we are lost. If I am walking, says Oehler, I am thinking and I maintain that I am walking, and suddenly I think and maintain that I am walking and thinking because that is what I am thinking while I am walking. And when we are walking together and *think* this thought, we think we are walking together, and suddenly we think, even if we don't think it together, we *are thinking*, but it is something different. If I think I am walking, it is something different from your thinking I am walking, just as it is something different if we both think at the same time (or simultaneously) that we are walking, if that is possible. Let's walk over the Friedensbrücke, I said earlier, says Oehler, and we walked over the Friedensbrücke because I thought I was thinking, I say, I am walking over the Friedensbrücke, I am walking with you so we are walking together over the Friedensbrücke. But it would be quite different were you to have had this thought, let's go over the Friedensbrücke, if you were to have thought, let's walk over the Friedensbrücke, and so on. When we are walking, intellectual movement comes with body movement. We always discover when we are walking, and so causing our body to start to move, that our thinking, which *was* not thinking in our head, also starts to move. We walk with our legs, we say, and think with our head. We could, however, also say we walk with our mind. Imagine walking in such an incredibly unstable state of mind, we think when we see someone walking whom we assume to be in that state of mind, as we think and say. This person is walking completely mindlessly, we say, just as we say, this mindless person is walking incredibly quickly or incredibly slowly or incredibly purposefully. Let's go, we say, into Franz Josef station when we know that we *are going to* say, let's go into Franz Josef station. Or we think we are saying let's walk over the Friedensbrücke and we walk over the Friedensbrücke because we have anticipated what we are doing, that is, walking over the Friedensbrücke. We think what we have anticipated and do what we have anticipated, says Oehler. After four or five minutes we intended to visit the park in Klosterneuburgerstrasse, the fact that we went into the park in Klosterneuburgerstrasse, says Oehler, presupposed that we *knew* for four or five minutes that we *would* go into the park in Klosterneuburgerstrasse. Just as when I say *let's go into Obenaus* it means that I have *thought, let's go into Obenaus,* irrespective of whether I go into Obenaus or not. But we are lost in thoughts like this, says Oehler, and it is pointless to occupy yourself with thoughts like this for any length of time. Thus we are always on the point of throwing away thoughts, throwing away the thoughts that we have and the thoughts that we always have, because we are in the habit of always having thoughts, throughout our lives, as far as we know, we throw thoughts away, we do nothing else because we are nothing but people who are always tipping out their minds like garbage cans and emptying them wherever they may be. If we have a head full of thoughts we tip our head out like a garbage can, says Oehler, but not everything onto one heap, says Oehler, but always in the place where we happen to be at a given moment. It is for this reason that the world is always full of a stench, because everybody is always emptying out their heads like a garbage can. Unless we find a different method, says Oehler, the world will, without doubt, one day be suffocated by the stench that this thought refuse generates. But it is improbable that there is any other method. All people fill their heads without thinking and without concern for others and they empty them where they like, says Oehler. It is this idea that I find the cruelest of all ideas. The person who thinks also thinks of his thinking as a form of walking, says Oehler. He says my or his or this train of thought. Thus it is absolutely right to say, let's enter this thought, just as if we were to say, let's enter this haunted house. Because we say it, says Oehler, because we have this idea, because we, as Karrer would have said, have this so-called idea of such a so-called train of thought. Let's go further (in thought), we say, when we want to develop a thought further, when we want to progress in a thought. This thought goes too far, and so on, is what is said. If we think that we have to go more quickly (or more slowly) we think that we have to think more quickly, although we know that thinking is not a question of speed, true it does deal with something, which is walking, when it is a question of walking, but thinking has nothing to do with speed, says Oehler. The difference between walking and thinking is that thinking has nothing to do with speed, but walking is actually always involved with speed. Thus, to say let's walk to Obenaus quickly or let's walk over the Friedensbrücke quickly is absolutely correct, but to say let's think faster, let's think quickly, is wrong, it is nonsense, and so on, says Oehler. When we are walking we are dealing with so-called practical concepts (in Karrer's words), when we are thinking we are dealing simply with concepts. But we can, of course, says Oehler, make thinking into walking and, vice versa, walking into thinking without departing from the fact that thinking has nothing to do with speed, walking everything. We can also say, over and over again, says Oehler, we have now walked to the end of such and such a road, it doesn't matter what road, whereas we can never say, now we have thought this thought to an end, there's no such thing and it is connected with the fact that walking but not thinking is connected with speed. Thinking is by no means speed, walking, quite simply, is speed. But underneath all this, as underneath everything, says Oehler, there is the world (and thus also the thinking) of practical or secondary concepts. We advance through the world of practical concepts or secondary concepts, but not through the world of concepts. In fact, we now intend to visit the park on Klosterneuburgerstrasse; after four or five minutes in the park on Klosterneuburgerstrasse, Oehler suddenly says, we still have some bird food we brought for the birds under the Friedensbrücke in our coat pockets. Do you have the bird food we brought for the birds under the Friedensbrücke in your coat pocket? To which I answer, yes. To our astonishment both of us, Oehler and I, still have, at this moment in the park on Klosterneuburgerstrasse, the bird food in our coat pockets that we brought for the birds under the Friedensbrücke. It is absolutely unusual, says Oehler, for us to forget to feed our bird food to the birds under the Friedensbrücke. Let's feed the birds our bird food now, says Oehler, and we feed the birds our bird food. We throw our bird food to the birds very quickly and the bird food is eaten up in a short time. These birds have a totally different, much more rapid, way of eating our bird food, says Oehler, different from the birds under the Friedensbrücke. Almost at the same moment, I also say: a totally different way. It was absolutely certain, I think, that I was ready to say the words in a totally different way before Oehler made his statement. We say something, says Oehler, and the other person maintains that he has just thought the same thing and was about to say what we had said. This peculiarity should be an occasion for us to busy ourselves with the peculiarity. But not today. I have never walked from the Friedensbrücke onto Klosterneuburgerstrasse so quickly, says Oehler. We, Karrer and I, also intended, says Oehler, to go straight from the Friedensbrücke back onto Klosterneuburgerstrasse, but no, we went into Rustenschacher's store, today I really don't know why we went into Rustenschacher's store but it's pointless to think about it. I can still hear myself saying, says Oehler, *let's go back onto Klosterneuburgerstrasse*. That is back to where we are now standing, because I always went walking with Karrer here, but certainly not to feed the birds, as I do with you. I can still hear myself saying, *let's go back onto Klosterneuburgerstrasse, we'll calm down on Klosterneuburgerstrasse*. I was already under the impression that what Karrer needed above all else was to calm down, his whole organism was at this moment nothing but sheer unrest: I really did call out to him several times, *let's go onto Klosterneuburgerstrasse*, that was what I said, but Karrer wasn't listening, I asked him to go to Klosterneuburgerstrasse, but Karrer wasn't listening, he suddenly stopped in front of Rustenschacher's store, a place I hate, says Oehler, the fact is that I hate Rustenschacher's store, and said, let's go into Rustenschacher's store and we went into Rustenschacher's store, although it was not, in the least, our intention to go into Rustenschacher's store, because when we were still in Franz Josef station we had said to one another, *today we will neither go to Obenaus nor into Rustenschacher's store*. I can still hear us both stating categorically *neither to Obenaus* (to drink our beer) *nor into Rustenschacher's store*, but suddenly we had gone into Rustenschacher's store, says Oehler, and what followed you know. What senselessness to reverse a decision, once taken, on the grounds of reason, as we had to say (afterwards) and replace it with what is often a terrible misfortune, says Oehler. I had never known such a hectic pace as when I was walking with Karrer down from the Friedensbrücke in the direction of Klosterneuburgerstrasse and into Rustenschacher's store, says Oehler. We had never even crossed the square in front of Franz Josef station so quickly. In spite of the people streaming towards us from Franz Josef station, in spite of these people suddenly streaming towards us, in spite of these hundreds of people suddenly streaming towards us, Karrer went towards Franz Josef station, and I thought that we would, as was his custom, sit down on one of the old benches intended for travelers, right in the midst of all the revolting dirt of Franz Josef station, as was his custom, says Oehler, to sit down on one of these benches and watch the people as they jump off the trains and as, in a short while, they start streaming all over the station, but no, shortly before we were going, as I thought, to enter the station and sit down on one of these benches, Karrer turns round and runs to the Friedensbrücke, runs, says Oehler several times, runs, past the "Railroader" clothing store towards the Friedensbrücke and from there into Rustenschacher's store at an unimaginable speed, says Oehler. Karrer actually ran away from Oehler. Oehler was only able to follow Karrer at a distance of more than ten, for a long while of fifteen or even twenty meters; while he was running along behind Karrer, Oehler kept thinking, if only Karrer doesn't go into Rustenschacher's store, *if only he won't be rash enough* to go into Rustenschacher's store, but precisely what Oehler feared, as he was running along behind Karrer, happened. Karrer said, *let's go into Rustenschacher's store*, and Karrer, without waiting for a word from Oehler, who was, by now, exhausted, went straight into Rustenschacher's store, Karrer tore open the door of Rustenschacher's store with an incredible vehemence, but was then able to pull himself together, says Oehler, only, of course, to lose control again immediately. Karrer ran to the counter, says Oehler, and the salesman, without arguing, began at once to show Karrer, to whom he had shown all the trousers the week before, all the trousers, to hold up all the trousers to the light. Look, said Karrer, says Oehler, his tone of voice suddenly so quiet, probably because we are now standing still, I have known this street from my childhood and I have been through everything that this street has been through, there is nothing in this street with which I would not be familiar, he, Karrer knew every regularity and every irregularity in this street, and even if it is one of the most ugly, he loved the street like no other. How often have I said to myself, said Karrer, you see these people day in day out, and it is always the same people whom you see and whom you know, always the same faces and always the same head and body movements as they walk, head and body movements that are characteristic of Klosterneuburgerstrasse. You know these hundreds and thousands of people, Karrer said to Oehler, and you know them, even if you do not know them, because basically they are always the same people, all these people are the same and they only differ in the eyes of the superficial observer (as judge). The way they walk and the way they do not walk and the way they shop and do not shop and the way they act in summer and the way they act in winter and the way they are born and the way they die, Karrer said to Oehler. You know all the terrible conditions. You know all the attempts (to live), those who do not emerge from these attempts, this whole attempt at life, this whole state of attempting, seen as a life, Karrer said to Oehler, says Oehler. You went to school here and you survived your father and your mother here, and others will survive you as you survived your father and mother, said Karrer to Oehler. It was on Klosterneuburgerstrasse that all the thoughts that ever occurred to you occurred to you (and if you know the truth, all your ideas, all your rebukes about your environment, your inner world they all occurred to you here). How many monstrosities is Klosterneuburgerstrasse filled with for you? You only need to go onto Klosterneuburgerstrasse, and all life's misery and all life's despair come at you. I think of these walls, these rooms with which, and in which, you grew up, the many illnesses characteristic of Klosterneuburgerstrasse, said Karrer, in Oehler's words, the dogs and the old people tied to the dogs. The way Karrer made these statements was, in Oehler's words, not surprising in the wake of Hollensteiner's suicide. Something hopeless, depressing, had taken hold of Karrer after Hollensteiner's death, something I had never observed in him before. Suddenly, everything took on the somber color of the person who sees nothing but *dying* and for whom nothing else seems to happen any more but only *the dying* that surrounds him. But Scherrer, according to Oehler, was not interested in all the changes in Karrer's personality that were connected with Hollensteiner's suicide. Do you remember how they dragged you into the entryway of these houses and how they boxed your ears in those entryways, Karrer suddenly says to me in a tone that absolutely shattered me. As if Hollensteiner's death had darkened the whole human or rather inhuman scene for him. How they beat up your mother and how they beat up your father, says Karrer, says Oehler. These hundreds and thousands of windows shut tight both summer and winter, says Karrer, according to Oehler, and he says it as hopelessly as possible. I shall never forget the days before the visit to Rustenschacher's store, says Oehler, how Karrer's condition got worse daily, how everything you had thought was already totally gloomy became gloomier and gloomier. The shouting and the collapsing and the silence on Klosterneuburgerstrasse that followed this shouting and collapsing, said Karrer, says Oehler. And this terrible filth! he says, as though there had never been anything in the world for him but filth. It was precisely the fact that everything on Klosterneuburgerstrasse, that everything remained as it always had been and that you had to fear, if you thought about it, that it would always remain the same and that had gradually made Klosterneuburgerstrasse into an enormous and insoluble problem for him. *Waking up and going to sleep on Klosterneuburgerstrasse,* Karrer kept repeating. *This incessant walking back and forth on Klosterneuburgerstrasse. My own helplessness and immobility on Klosterneuburgerstrasse.* In the last two days these statements and scraps of statements had continually repeated themselves, says Oehler. *We have absolutely no ability to leave Klosterneuburgerstrasse. We have no power to make decisions any more. What we are doing is nothing. What we breathe is nothing. When we walk, we walk from one hopelessness to another. We walk and we always walk into a still more hopeless hopelessness. Walking away, nothing but walking away,* says Karrer, according to Oehler, over and over again. *Nothing but walking away. All those years I thought I would alter something, and that means everything, and walk away from Klosterneuburgerstrasse, but nothing changed* (because he changed nothing), says Oehler, and he did not go away. *If you do not walk away early enough,* said Karrer, *it is suddenly too late and you can no longer walk away. It is suddenly clear you can do what you like, but you can no longer walk away.*

No longer being able to alter this problem of not being able to walk away any more occupies your whole life, Karrer is supposed to have said, and from then on that is all that occupies your life. You then grow more and more helpless and weaker and weaker and all you keep saying to yourself is that you should have walked away early enough, and you ask yourself why you did not walk away early enough. But when we ask ourselves why we did not walk away and why we did not walk away early enough, which means did not walk away at the moment when it was *high time* to do so, we understand nothing more, said Karrer to Oehler. Oehler says: because we did not think intensively enough about changing things when we really should have thought intensively about making changes and in fact did think intensively about making changes, but not intensively enough because we did not think intensively in the most inhuman way about making changes in something, and that means, above all, ourselves, making changes in ourselves to change ourselves and by this means to change everything, said Karrer. The circumstances were always such as to make it impossible for us. Circumstances are everything, we are nothing, said Karrer. What sort of states and what sort of circumstances have I been in, in which I simply have not been able to change myself in all these years because it all boiled down to a question of states and circumstances that could not be changed, said Karrer. Thirty years ago, when you, Oehler, went off to America, where, as I know, most circumstances were really dreadful, Karrer is supposed to have said, I should have left Klosterneuburgerstrasse, but I did not leave it; now I feel this whole humiliation as a truly horrible punishment. Our whole life is composed of nothing but terrible and, at the same time, terrifying circumstances (as states), and if you take life apart it simply disintegrates into frightful circumstances and states, Karrer said to Oehler. And when you are on a street like this for so long a time, so long that you have left the discovery that you have grown old behind you long ago, you can, of course, no longer walk away, in thought yes, but in reality no, but to walk away in thought and not in reality means a double torment, said Karrer, after you are forty, your willpower itself is already so weakened that it is senseless even to attempt to walk away. A street like Klosterneuburgerstrasse is, for a person of my age, a sealed tomb from which you hear nothing but dreadful things, said Karrer. Karrer is supposed to have said the words *the vicious process of dying* several times, and several times *early ruin*. How I hated these houses, Karrer is supposed to have said, and yet I kept on going into these houses with a lifelong appetite that is nothing short of depressing. All these hundreds and thousands of mentally sick people who have come out of these houses dead over the course of those years, said Karrer. For every dreadful person who has died from one of these houses, two or three new dreadful people are *created into* these houses, Karrer is supposed to have said to Oehler. I haven't been into Rustenschacher's store for weeks, Karrer said the day before he went into Rustenschacher's store, says Oehler. We live in a time when one should be at least twenty or thirty years younger if one is to survive, Karrer said to Oehler. There has never been an artificiality like it, an artificiality with such a naturalness, for which one should not be over forty. No matter where you look, you are looking into artificiality, said Karrer. Two or three years ago, this street was still not so artificial that it terrified me. But I cannot explain this artificiality, said Karrer. Just as I cannot explain anything any more, said Karrer. Filth and age and absolute artificiality, said Karrer. You with your Ferdinand Ebner, Karrer kept on repeating, and I, at first, with my Wittgenstein, then you with your Wittgenstein and I with my Ferdinand Ebner. When in addition one is dependent upon a female person, my sister, said Karrer. But it is frightful after years of absence, suddenly to face all these people (in Obenaus), said Karrer. If things are peaceful around me, then I am restless, the more restless I grow, the more peaceful things are around me, and vice versa, said Karrer. When you are suddenly dragged back into your filth, said Karrer. Into the filth that has doubtless increased in the thirty years, said Karrer. After thirty years it is a much filthier filth than it was thirty years ago, says Karrer. When I am lying in bed, assuming that my sister keeps quiet, that she is not pacing up and down in her room, which is opposite mine, said Karrer, that she is not, as she is in the habit of doing just as I have gone to bed, opening up all the cupboards and all the chests and suddenly clearing out all these cupboards and chests, then I think back on what I was thinking the day before, said Karrer. I close my eyes and lay the palms of my hands on the blanket and go back very intensely over the previous day. With a constantly increasing intensity, with an intensity that can constantly be increased. The intensity can always be increased, it may be that this exercise will one day cross the border into madness, but I cannot be bothered about that, said Karrer. The time when I did bother about it is past, I do not bother about it any more, said Karrer. The state of complete indifference, in which I then find myself, said Karrer, is, through and through, a philosophical state.